D0923570

BRIDGING THE GALAXIES

BRIDGING THE GALAXIES

BY

LARRY NIVEN

ILLUSTRATIONS BY

ALICIA AUSTIN

SAN FRANCISCO SCIENCE
FICTION CONVENTIONS, INC.
1993

Bridging the Galaxies

Printed in the United States of America.

Cover and all interior illustrations by Alicia Austin
Starburst typeface designed by David Rakowski
Design and production by Catherine Campaigne

TABLE OF CONTENTS

INTRODUCTION

BY LARRY NIVEN

I'm a dilettante.

It took me a while to admit that to myself. Hah! You thought I was a professional, didn't you? Nope. I have to wait for inspiration. I give inspiration every chance—I keep current on all the interesting sciences, go to AAAS meetings and so forth—and when inspiration hits, I follow it.

Sometimes I can publish the result.

"Procrustes" is the sixth Beowulf Shaeffer story. The previous Beowulf Shaeffer story won me my last Hugo Award, seventeen years ago. He's my favorite character type: the tourist too lazy to keep himself out of trouble. I thought he was gone for good.

"The Léshy Circuit" has never appeared in print. The intent was to create a planetarium show: the kind of story that is projected on the dome of a planetarium. The basic restriction is, no actors. Just still pictures, or moving starscapes, and voice-overs. I wrote several of these for Hansen Planetarium in Salt Lake City, at their suggestion, before I realized the truth: I was showing them what their taboos are, by breaking them.

I wrote "It's Only a Story" for a theme anthology, for Greens who *really* want to save the planet.

Jerry Pournelle and I wrote "Where Next, Columbus?"

for *Smithsonian Magazine* and the Columbus half-millenium.

Reason Magazine commissioned "Tabletop Fusion," and paid for it, and would have published it if the world hadn't lost faith in cold fusion.

I wrote "Intercon Trip Report" because it was so much fun . . . and because I write a lot of letters.

I wrote "The South Los Angeles Broadcasting System" because some people burned down half my city. I don't believe I'm finished with that subject.

"The Color of Sunfire" has never been published, and the reason is that the ideas were used in other stories, particularly *Ringworld.* But it does wrap up the story begun in "A Relic of the Empire."

"All the Bridges Rusting" is kind of an orphan. I wrote five stories of the JumpShift or "Flash Crowd" universe, in which teleportation is being invented about, oh, now. Four were crime stories, more or less. "Bridges" was intended as classic *Analog*, and it's here because it fits the theme of the convention.

My intent in this book was to demonstrate some versatility. It would be quite different, if Tor had not published two books a couple of years ago. *N-Space* and *Playgrounds of the Mind* include some stuff I never expected to see in print, unless in fanzines.

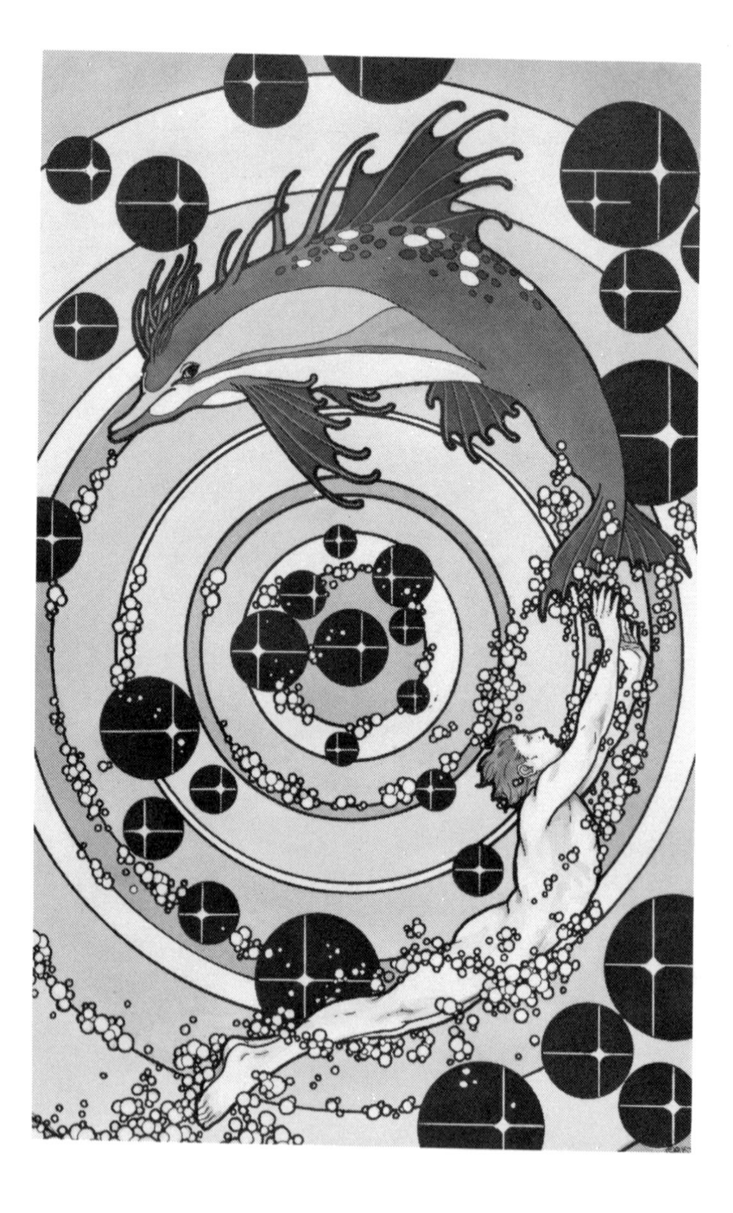

PROCRUSTES

Asleep, my mind plays it all back in fragments and dreams. From time to time a block of nerves wakes: *That's some kind of ARM weapon! Move it move it too late BLAM. My head rolls loose on black sand. Bones shattered, ribs and spine. Fear worse than the agony. Agony fading* and I'm gone.

Legs try to kick. Nothing moves. Again, harder, *move! No go. The 'doc floats nicely on the lift plate, but its mass is resisting me. Push! Voice behind me, I turn, she's holding some kind of tube. BLAM. My head bounces on sand. Agony flaring, sensation fading. Try to hang on, stay lucid . . . but everything turns mellow.*

My balance swings wildly around my inner ear. *Where's the planet's axis? Fafnir doesn't have polar caps. The ancient lander is flying itself. Carlos looks worried, but Feather's having the time of her life.*

Sprawled across the planet's face, a hurricane flattened along one edge. Under the vast cloud-fingerprint a ruddy snake divides the blue of a world-girdling ocean. A long, narrow continent runs almost pole to pole.

The lander re-enters over featureless ocean. Nothing down there seems to be looking at us. I'm taking us down fast. Larger islands have low, flat buildings on them. Pick a little one. Hover while flame digs the lamplighter pit wider and deeper, until the lander sinks into the hole with inches to spare. Plan A is right on track.

I remember how Plan A ended. The Surgeon program senses my distress and turns me off.

I'm in Carlos Wu's 'doc, in the Intensive Care Cavity. The Surgeon program prods my brain, running me through my memories, maintaining the patterns, lest they fuzz out to nothing while my brain and body heal.

I must be terribly damaged.

Waking was sudden. My eyes popped open and I was on my back, my nose two inches from glass. Sunlight glared through scattered clouds. Display lights glowed above my eyebrows. I felt fine, charged with energy.

Ye gods, how long had I slept? All those dreams ... dream-memories.

I tried to move. I was shrink-wrapped in elastic. I wiggled my arm up across my chest, with considerable effort, and up to the displays. It took me a few seconds to figure them out.

Biomass tank: near empty. *Treatment:* pages of data, horrifying ... terminated, successful. Date: Omygod. Four months! I was out for four months and eleven days!

I typed, *Open:*

The dark glass lid retracted, sunlight flared, and I shut my eyes tight. After a while I pulled myself over the rim of the Intensive Care Cavity and rolled out.

My balance was all wrong. I landed like a lumpy sack, on sand, and managed not to yell or swear. Who might hear? Sat up, squinting painfully, and looked around.

I was still on the island.

It was weathered coral, nearly symmetrical, with a central

peak. The air was sparkling clear and the ocean went on forever, with another pair of tiny islands just touching the horizon.

I was stark naked and white as a bone, in the glare of a yellow-white dwarf sun. The air was salty and thick with organic life, sea life.

Where was everybody?

I tried to stand; wobbled; gave it up and crawled around into the shadow of the 'doc. I still felt an amazing sense of well-being, as if I could solve anything the universe could throw at me.

During moments of half-wakefulness I'd somehow worked out where I must be. Here it stood, half coffin and half chemical lab, massive and abandoned on the narrow black sand beach. A vulnerable place to leave such a valuable thing; but this was where I'd last seen it, ready to be loaded into the boat.

Sunlight could damage me in minutes, kill me in hours; but Carlos Wu's wonderful 'doc was no ordinary Mall autodoctor. It was state-of-the-art, smarter than me in some respects. It would cure anything the sun could do to me.

I pulled myself to my feet and took a few steps. Ouch! The coral cut my feet. The 'doc could cure that too, but it hurt.

Standing, I could see most of the island. The center bulged up like a volcano. Fafnir coral builds a flat island with a shallow cone rising at the center, a housing for a symbiote, the lamplighter. I'd hovered the lander above the cone while belly jets scorched out the lamplighter nest, until it was big enough to hold the lander.

Just me and the 'doc and a dead island. I'd have to live in the 'doc. Come out at night, like a vampire. My chance of being found must be poor, if no passing boat had found me in these past four-plus months.

I climbed. The coral cut my hands and feet, and knees. From the cone I'd be able to see the whole island.

The pit was two hundred feet across. The bottom was black and smooth, and seven or eight feet below me. Feather had set the lander to melt itself down, slowly, radiating not much heat over many hours. Several inches of rainwater now covered the slag, and something sprawled in the muck.

It might be a man ... a tall man, possibly raised in low gravity. Too tall to be Carlos. Or Sharrol, or Feather, and who was left?

I jumped down. Landed clumsily on the smooth slag and splashed full length in the water. Picked myself up, unhurt. My toes could feel an oblong texture, lines and ridges, the shapes within the lander that wouldn't melt. Police could determine what this thing had been, if they ever looked; but why would they look?

The water felt good on my ruined feet. And on my skin. I was already burned. Albinos can't take yellow dwarf sunlight.

A corpse was no surprise, given what I remembered. I looked it over. It had been wearing local clothing for a man: boots, loose pants with a rope tie, a jacket encrusted with pockets. The jacket was pierced with a great ragged hole front and back. That could only have been made by Feather's horrible ARM weapon. This close, the head.... I'd thought it must be under the water, but there was no head at all. There were clean white bones, and a neck vertebra cut smoothly in half.

I was hyperventilating. Dizzy. I sat down next to the skeleton so that I wouldn't fall.

These long bones looked more than four months dead. Years, decades ... wait, now. We'd scorched the nest, but there would be lamplighter soldiers left outside. Those would have swarmed down and stripped the bones.

I found I was trying to push my back through a wall of fused coral. My empty stomach heaved. This was much worse than anything I'd imagined. I knew who this was.

Sunlight burned my back. My eyes were going wonky in the glare. Time was not on my side: I was going to be much sicker much quicker than I liked.

I made myself pull the boots loose, shook the bones out and put them on. They were too big.

The jacket was a sailor's survival jacket, local style. The shoulders looked padded: shoulder floats. The front and sides had been all pockets, well stuffed; but front and back had been torn to confetti.

I stripped it off him and began searching pockets.

No wallet, no ID. Tissue pack. The shrapnel remains of a hand computer. Several pockets were sealed: emergency gear, stuff you wouldn't want to open by accident; some of those had survived.

A knife of exquisite sharpness in a built-in holster. Pocket torch. A ration brick. I bit into the brick and chewed while I searched. Mag specs, one lens shattered, but I put them on anyway. Without dark glasses my pink albino eyes would go blind.

Sun block spray, unharmed: good. A pill dispenser, broken, but in a pocket still airtight. Better! Tannin secretion pills!

The boots were shrinking, adapting to my feet. It felt friendly, reassuring. My most intimate friends on this island.

I was still dizzy. Better let the 'doc take care of me now; take the pills afterward. I shook broken ribs out of the jacket. Shook the pants empty. Balled the clothing and tossed it out of the hole. Tried to follow it.

My fingers wouldn't reach the rim.

"After all this, what a stupid way to die," I said to the memory of Sharrol Janz. "What do I do now? Build a ladder out of bones?" If I got out of this hole, I'd think it through before I ever did *anything*.

I knelt; I yelled and jumped. My fingers, palms, forearms gripped rough coral. I pulled myself out and lay panting, sweating, bleeding, crying.

I limped back to the 'doc, wearing boots now, holding the suit spread above me for a parasol. I was feverish with sunburn.

I couldn't take boots into the ICC. *Wait. Think. Wind? Waves?* I tied the clothes in a bundle around the boots, and set it on the 'doc next to the faceplate. I climbed into the Intensive Care Cavity and pulled the lid down.

Sharrol would wait an hour longer, if she was still alive. And the kids. And Carlos.

I did not expect to fall asleep.

❁

Asleep, feverish with sunburn. The Surgeon program tickles blocks of nerves, plays me like a complex toy. In my sleep I feel raging thirst, hear a thunderclap, taste cinnamon or coffee, clench a phantom fist.

My skin wakes. Piloerection runs in ripples along my body, then a universal tickle, then pressure ... like that feather-crested snakeskin Sharrol put me into for Carlos's party....

❁

Sharrol, sliding into her own rainbow-scaled body suit, stopped halfway. "You don't really want to do this, do you?"

"I'll tough it out. How do I look?" I'd never developed the least sense of flatlander style. Sharrol picked my clothes.

"Half man, half snake," she said. "Me?"

"Like this snake's fitting mate." She didn't really. No flatlander is as supple as a crashlander. Raised in Earth's gravity, Sharrol was a foot shorter than I, and weighed the same as I did. Stocky.

The apartment was already in child mode: rounded surfaces everywhere, and all storage was locked or raised to eyeball height (mine). Tanya was five and Louis was four and both were agile as monkeys. I scanned for anything that might be dangerous within their reach.

Louis stared at us, solemn, awed. Tanya giggled. We must have looked odder than usual, though given flatlander styles, it's a wonder that any kid can recognize its parents. Why do they change their hair and skin color so often? When we hugged them goodbye Tanya made a game of tugging my hair out of shape and watching it flow back into a feathery crest. We set them down and turned on the Playmate program.

The lobby transfer booth jumped us three time zones east. We stepped out into a vestibule, facing an arc of picture window. A flock of rainbow-hued fish panicked at the awful sight and flicked away. A huge fish passed in some internal dream.

For an instant I felt the weight of all those tons of water. I looked to see how Sharrol was taking it. She was smiling, admiring.

"Carlos lives near the Great Barrier Reef, you said. You didn't say he lived in it."

"It's a great privilege," Sharrol told me. "I spent my first thirty years under water, but not on the Reef. The Reef's too fragile. The UN protects it."

"You never told me that!"

She grinned at my surprise. "My Dad had a lobster ranch near Boston. Later I worked for the Epcot-Atlantis police. The ecology isn't so fragile there, but—Bey, I should take you there."

I said, "Maybe it's why we think alike. I grew up underground. You can't build above ground on We Made It."

"You told me. The winds."

"Sharrol, this isn't like Carlos."

She'd known Carlos Wu years longer than I had. "Carlos gets an idea and he follows it as far as it'll go. I don't know what he's onto now. Maybe he's always wanted to share me with you. And he brought a date for, um—"

"Ever met her?"

"—balance. No, Carlos won't even talk about Feather Filip. He just smiles mysteriously. Maybe it's love."

The children! Protect the children! Where are the children? The Surgeon must be tickling my adrenal glands. I'm not awake, but I'm frantic, and a bit randy too. Then the sensations ease off. *The Playmate program. It guards them and teaches them and plays with them. They'll be fine. Can't take them to Carlos's place … not tonight.*

Sharrol was their mother and Carlos Wu had been their father. Earth's Fertility Board won't let an albino have children. Carlos's gene pattern they judge perfect; he's one of a hundred and twenty flatlanders who carry an unlimited birthright.

A man can love any child. That's hard-wired into the brain. A man can raise another man's children. And accept their father as a friend . . . but there's a barrier. That's wired in too.

Sharrol knows. She's afraid I'll turn prickly and uncivilized. And *Carlos* knows. So why. . .?

Tonight was billed as a foursome, sex and *tapas.* That was a developing custom: dinner strung out as a sequence of small dishes between bouts of recreational sex. Something inherited from the ancient Greeks or Italians, maybe. There's something lovers gain from feeding each other.

Feather—

The memory blurs. I wasn't afraid of her then, but I am now. When I remember Feather, the Surgeon puts me to sleep.

But the children! I've got to remember. We were down. Sharrol was out of the 'doc, but we left Louis and Tanya frozen. We floated their box into the boat. Feather and I disengaged the lift plate and slid it under the 'doc. Beneath that lumpy jacket she moved like a tigress. She spoke my name; I turned. . . .

Feather.

Carlos's sleepfield enclosed most of the bedroom. He'd hosted bigger parties than this in here. Tonight we were down to four, and a floating chaos of dishes Carlos said were Mexican.

"She's an ARM," Carlos said.

Feather Filip and I were sharing a tamale too spicy for Sharrol. Feather caught me staring and grinned back. An ARM?

I'd expected Feather to be striking. She wasn't exactly beautiful. She was strong: lean, almost gaunt, with prominent tendons in her neck, lumps flexing at the corners of her jaws. You don't get strength like that without training in illegal martial arts.

The Amalgamated Regional Militia is the United Nations

police, and the United Nations took a powerful interest in Carlos Wu. What was she, Carlos's bodyguard? Was that how they'd met?

But whenever one of us spoke of the ARM that afternoon, Feather changed the subject.

I'd have thought Carlos would orchestrate our sleepfield dance. Certified genius that he is, would he not be superb at that too? But Feather had her own ideas, and Carlos let her lead. Her lovemaking was aggressive and acrobatic. I felt her strength, that afternoon. And my own lack, raised as I was in the lower gravity of We Made It.

And three hours passed in that fashion, while the wonderful colors of the reef darkened to light-amplified night.

And then Feather reached far out of the field, limber as a snake . . . reached inside her backpurse, and fiddled, and frowned, and rolled back and said, "We're shielded."

Carlos said, "They'll know."

"They know *me*," Feather said. "They're thinking that I let them use their monitors because I'm showing off, but now we're going to try something a little kinky. Or maybe I'm just putting them on. I've done it before—"

"Then—"

"—Find a glitch so I can block their gear with something new. Then they fix it. They'll fix this one too, but not tonight. It's just Feather coming down after a long week."

Carlos accepted that. "Stet. Sharrol, Beowulf, do you want to leave Earth? We'd be traveling as a group, Louis and Tanya and the four of us. This is for keeps."

Sharrol said, "I can't." Carlos knew that.

He said, "You can ride in cold sleep. Home's rotation

period is six minutes shorter than Earth's. Mass the same, air about the same. Tectonic activity is higher, so it'll smell like there's just a trace of smog—"

"Carlos, we talked this to death a few years ago." Sharrol was annoyed. "Sure, I could live on Home. I don't like the notion of flying from world to world like a, a corpse, but I'd do it. But the UN doesn't want me emigrating, and Home won't take flat phobes!"

The flatlander phobia is a bone-deep dread of being cut off from the Earth. Fear of flying and/or falling is an extreme case, but no flat phobe can travel in space. You find few flat phobes off Earth; in fact, Earthborn are called flatlanders no matter how well they adjust to life elsewhere.

But Feather was grinning at Sharrol. "We go by way of Fafnir. We'll get to Home as Shashters. Home has already approved us for immigration—"

"Under the name *Graynor.* We're all married," Carlos amplified.

I said, "Carlos, you've *been* off Earth. You were on Jinx for a year."

"Yah. Bey, Sigmund Ausfaller and his gnomes never lost track of me. The United Nations thinks they own my genes. I'm supervised wherever I go."

But they keep you in luxury, I thought. And the grass is always greener. Feather had her own complaint. "What do you know about the ARM?" she asked us.

"We listen to the vid," Sharrol said.

"Sharrol, dear, we *vet* that stuff. The ARM decides what you don't get to know about us. Most of us take psychoactive chemicals to keep us in a properly paranoid mindframe during working hours. We stay that way four days, then go sane for the weekend. If it's making us too crazy, they retire us."

Feather was nervous and trying to restrain it, but now hard-edged muscles flexed, and her elbows and knees were pulling in protectively against her torso. "But some of us are born this way. We go *off* chemicals when we go to work. The 'doc doses us back to sanity Thursday afternoon. I've been an ARM schiz for thirty-five years. They're ready to retire me, but they'd never let me go to some other world, knowing what I know. And they don't want a schiz making babies."

I didn't say that I could see their point. I looked at Sharrol and saw hope in the set of her mouth, ready to smile but holding off. We were being brought into these plans *way* late. Rising hackles had pulled me right out of any postcoital glow.

Feather told me, "They'll never let you go either, Beowulf."

And *that* was nonsense. "Feather, I've been off Earth three times since I got here."

"Don't try for four. You know too much. You know about the Core explosion, and diplomatic matters involving alien races—"

"I've left Earth since—"

"—and Julian Forward's work." She gave it a dramatic pause. "We'll have some advanced weaponry out of that. We would not want the kzinti to know about that, or the trinocs, or certain human domains. That last trip, do you know how much *talking* you did while you were on Gummidgy and Jinx? You're a friendly, talkative guy with great stories, Beowulf!"

I shrugged. "So why trust me with this? Why didn't you and Carlos just go?"

She gestured at Carlos. He grinned and said, "I insisted."

"And we need a pilot," Feather said. "That's you, Beowulf.

But I can bust us loose. I've set up something nobody but an ARM would ever dream of."

She told us about it.

To the kzinti the world was only a number. Kzinti don't like ocean sports. The continent was Shasht, "Burrowing Murder." Shasht was nearly lifeless, but the air was breathable and the mines were valuable. The kzinti had dredged up megatons of seabottom to fertilize a hunting jungle, and they got as far as seeding and planting before the Fourth Man-Kzin War.

After the war humankind took Shasht as reparations, and named the world *Fafnir.*

On Fafnir Feather's investigations found a family of six: two men, two women, two children. The Graynors were ready to emigrate.

Local law would cause them to leave most of their wealth behind, but then, they'd lost most of it already, backing some kind of recreational facilities on the continent.

"I've recorded them twice. The Graynors'll find funding waiting for them at Wunderland. They won't talk. The *other* Graynor family will emigrate to Home—"

"That's us?"

Feather nodded. Carlos said, "But if you and the kids won't come, Feather'll have to find someone else."

I said, "Carlos, *you'll* be watched. I don't supposed Feather can protect you from that."

"No. Feather's taken a much bigger risk—"

"They'll never miss it." She turned to me. "I got hold of a little stealth lander, Fourth War vintage, with a cold sleep box in back for you, Sharrol. We'll take that down to Fafnir. I've got an inflatable boat to take us to the Shasht North spaceport, and we'll get to Home on an Outbound Enterprises iceliner. Sharrol, you'll board the liner already frozen; I know how to bypass that stage." Feather was excited now. She gripped my arm and said, "We have to go get the lander, Beowulf. It's on Mars."

Sharrol said, "Tanya's a flat phobe too."

Feather's fingers closed with bruising force. I sensed that the lady didn't like seeing her plans altered.

"Wait one," Carlos said. "We can fix that. We're taking my 'doc, aren't we? It wouldn't be *plausible*, let alone intelligent, for Carlos Wu to go on vacation without his 'doc. Feather, how big is the lander's freezebox?"

"Yeah. Right. It'll hold Tanya ... better yet, both children. Sharrol can ride in your 'doc."

We talked it around. When we were satisfied, we went home.

Three days out, three days returning, and a week on Mars while the ARM team played with the spacecraft *Boy George*. It had to be Feather and me. I would familiarize myself with *Boy George*, Feather would supervise the ARM crews ... and neither of us were flat phobes.

I bought a dime disk, a tourist's guide of Fafnir system, and I studied it.

Kzinti and human planetologists call Fafnir a typical water world in a system older than Sol. The system didn't actually retain much more water than Earth did; that isn't the problem. But the core is low in radioactives. The lithosphere is thick: no continental drift here. Shallow oceans cover 93% of the planet. The oceans seethe with life, five billion years evolved, twice as old as Earth's.

And, where the thick crust cracked in early days, magma oozed through to build the world's single continent. Today a wandering line of volcanoes and bare rock stretches from the south pole nearly to the north. The continent's mass has been growing for billions of years.

On the opposite face of a lopsided planet, the ocean has grown shallow. Fafnir's life presently discovered the advantages of coral building. That side of the world is covered with tens of thousands of coral islands. Some stand up to twenty meters tall: relics of a deeper ocean.

The mines are all on Shasht. So also are all the industry, both spaceports, and the seat of government. But the life—recreation, housing, families—are all on the islands.

✺

Finding the old lander had indeed been a stroke of luck. It was an identical backup for the craft that set Sinbad Jabar down on Meerowsk in the Fourth War, where he invaded the harem of the Patriarch's Voice. The disgrace caused the balance of power among the local kzinti to become unstable. The human alliance took Meerowsk and renamed the planet, and it was Jabar's Prize until a later, pacifist generation took power. Jabar's skin is displayed there still.

Somehow Feather had convinced the ARMs that first, this twin of Jabar's lander was wanted for the Smithsonian Luna, and second, the Belt peoples would raise hell if they knew it was to be removed from Mars. The project must be absolutely secret.

Ultimately the ARM crews grew tired of Feather's supervision, or else her company. Rapidly after that, Feather grew tired of watching me read. "We'll only be on Fafnir two days, Beowulf. What are you learning? It's a dull, dull, dull place. All the land life is Earth imports—"

"Their lifestyle is strange, Feather. They travel by transfer booths and dirigible balloons and boats, and almost nothing in between. A very laid-back society. Nobody's expected to be anywhere on time—"

"Nobody's watching us here. You don't have to play tourist."

"I know." If the ARM had *Boy George* bugged . . . but Feather would have thought of *that.*

Our ship was in the hands of ARM engineers, and that made for tension. But we were getting on each other's nerves. Not a good sign, with a three-week flight facing us.

Feather said, "You're not playing. You are a tourist!"

I admitted it. "And the first law of tourism is, *read everything.*" But I switched the screen off and said, in the spirit of compromise, "All right. Show me. What is there to see on Mars?"

She hated to admit it. "Nothing."

We left Mars with the little stealth lander in the fuel tank. The ARM was doing things the ARM didn't know about. And I continued reading. . . .

Fafnir's twenty-two-hour day has encouraged an active life. Couch potatoes court insomnia: It's easier to sleep if you're tired.

But *hurrying* is something else. There are transfer booths, of course. You can jump instantly from a home on some coral extrusion to the bare rock of Shasht . . . and buy yourself an eleven-hour time lag.

Nobody's in a hurry to go home. They go by dirigible. Ultimately the floatliner companies wised up and began selling round trip tickets for the same price as one way.

"I do *know* all this, Beowulf."

"Mph? Oh, good."

"So what's the plan?" Feather asked. "Find an island with nothing near it and put down, right? Get out and dance around on the sand while we blow the boat up and load it and go. How do we hide the lander?"

"Sink it."

"Read about lamplighters," she said, so I did.

After the war and the settlement, UN Advance Forces landed on Shasht, took over the kzinti structures, then began to explore. Halfway around the planet were myriads of little round coral islands, each with a little peak at the center. At night the peaks glowed with a steady yellow light. Larger islands were chains of peaks, each with its yellow glow in the cup. Lamplighters were named before anyone knew what they were.

Close up . . . well, they've been called piranha ant nests. The bioluminescence attracts scores of varieties of flying fish. Or, lured or just lost, a swimming thing may beach itself; and then the lamplighter horde flows down to the beach and cleans it to the bones.

You can't build a home, or beach a boat, until the nest has been burned out. *Then* you have to wait another twelve days for the soldiers caught outside the nest to die. *Then* cover the nest. Use it for a basement, put your house on it. Otherwise the sea may carry a queen to you, to use the nest again.

"You're ahead of me on this," I admitted. "What has this lander got for belly rockets?"

"Your basic hydrogen and oxygen," Feather said. "High heat and a water vapor exhaust. We'll burn the nest out."

"Good."

Yo! Boy, when Carlos's 'doc is finished with you, you know it!

Open.

The sky was a brilliant sprawl of stars, some of them moving—spacecraft, weather eyes, the wheel—and a single lopsided moon. The island was shadow-teeth cutting into the starscape. I slid out carefully, into a blackness like the inside of my empty belly, and yelled as I dropped into seawater.

The water was hip deep, with no current to speak of. I wasn't going to drown, or be washed away, or lost. Fafnir's moon was a little one, close in. Tides would be shallow.

Still I'd been lucky: I could have wakened under water.

How did people feel about nudity here? But my bundle of clothes hadn't washed away. Now the boots clasped my feet like old friends. The sleeves of the dead man's survival jacket trailed way past my hands until I rolled them up, and of course the front and back were in shreds. The pants were better: too big, but with elastic ankle bands that I just pulled up to my knees. I swallowed a tannin secretion dose. I couldn't do that earlier. The 'doc would have read the albino gene in my DNA and "cured" me of an imposed tendency to tan.

There was nothing on all of Fafnir like Carlos's 'doc. I'd have to hide it before I could ever think about rescue.

"Our medical equipment," Carlos had called it; and Feather had answered, "Hardly ours."

Carlos was patient. "It's all we've got, Feather. Let me show you how to use it. First, the diagnostics."

The thing was as massive as the inflatable boat that would carry us to Shasht. Carlos had a gravity lift to shove under it. The Intensive Care Cavity was tailored just for Carlos Wu, naturally, but any of us could be served by the tethers and sleeves and hypo-tipped tubes and readouts along one whole face of the thing: the service wall.

"These hookups do your diagnostics and set the chemical feeds going. Feather, it'll rebalance body chemistry, in case I ever go schiz or someone poisons me or something. I've reprogrammed it to take care of you too." I don't think Carlos noticed the way Feather looked at it, and him.

"Now the cavity. It's for the most serious injuries, but I've reprogrammed it for you, Sharrol my dear—"

"But it's exactly Carlos's size," Feather told us pointedly. "The UN thinks a lot of Carlos. *We* can't use it."

Sharrol said, "It looks small. I don't mean the ICC cavity. I can get into that. But there's not much room for transplants in that storage space."

"Oh, no. This is advanced stuff. I had a hand in the design. One day we'll be able to use these techniques with everyone."

Carlos patted the monster. "There's nothing in here in the way of cloned organs and such. There's the Surgeon program, and a reservoir of organic soup, and a googol of self-replicating machines a few hundred atoms long. If I lost a leg or an eye, they'd turn me off and rebuild it onto me. There's even . . . here, pay attention. You feed the organics reservoir through here, so the machine doesn't run out of material. You could even feed it Fafnir fish if you can catch them, but they're metal-deficient. . . ."

When he had us thoroughly familiar with the beast, he helped Sharrol into the cavity, waited to be sure she was hooked up, and closed it. That made me nervous as hell. She climbed out a day later claiming that she hadn't felt a thing, wasn't hungry, didn't even have to use the bathroom.

The 'doc was massive. I had to really heave against it to get it moving, and then it wanted to move along the shore. I forced it to turn inland. The proper place to hide it was in the lamplighter nest, of course.

I was gasping like death itself, and the daylight had almost died, and I just couldn't push that mass uphill.

I left it on the beach. Maybe there was an answer. Let my hindbrain toy with it for awhile.

I trudged across sand to rough coral and kept walking to the peak. We'd picked the island partly for its isolation. Two distant yellow lights, eastward, marked two islands I'd noted earlier. I ran my mag specs (the side that worked) up to 20X and scanned the whole horizon, and found nothing but the twin lamplighter glows.

And nothing to do but wait.

I sat with my back against the lip of the dead lamplighter pit. I pictured her: She looked serious, a touch worried, under a feather crest and undyed skin; pink shading to brown, an Anglo tanned as if by Fafnir's yellow-white sun.

I said, "Sharrol."

Like the dead she had slept, her face slack beneath the faceplate, like Sleeping Beauty. I'd taken to talking to her, wondering if some part of her heard. I'd never had the chance to ask.

"I never wondered why you loved me. Egotist, I am. But, you must have looked like me when you were younger. Thirty years underwater, no sunlight. Your uncles, your father, they must have looked a *lot* like me. Maybe even with white hair. How old *are* you? I never asked."

Her memory looked at me.

"Tanj that. *Where* are you? Where are Tanya and Louis? Where's Carlos? What happened after I was shot?"

Faint smile, shrug of eyebrows.

"You spent three weeks unconscious in the ICC followed by ten minutes on your feet. Wrong gravity, wrong air mix, wrong smells. We hit you with everything it might take to knock a flat phobe spinning. Then BLAM and your love interest is lying on the sand with a hole through him.

"Maybe you tried to kill her. I don't think you'd give her much trouble, but maybe Feather would kill you anyway. She'd still have the kids. . . ."

I slammed my fist on coral. "What did she *want?* That crazy woman. I never hurt her at all."

Talking to Sharrol: Lifeless as she was, maybe it wasn't quite as *crazy* as talking to myself. I couldn't talk to the others. They—"You remember that night we planned it all? Feather was lucid then. Comparatively. We were there for her as *people.* On the trip to Mars she was a lot wilder. She was a hell of an *active* lover, but I never really got the feeling that I was *there* for her."

We never talked about each other's lovers. In truth, it was easier to say these things to Sharrol when she wasn't here.

"But most of the way to Fafnir, Feather was fine. But she wasn't sleeping with me. Just Carlos. She could hold a conversation, no problem there, but I was *randy*, love, and frustrated. She liked that. I caught a *look* when Carlos wasn't looking. So I didn't want to talk to her. And she was always up against Carlos, and Carlos, he was a bit embarrassed about it all. We talked about plans, but for anything personal there was just you. Sleeping Beauty."

The night was warm and clear. By convention, boats would show any color except lamplighter yellow. I couldn't miss seeing a boat's lights.

"Then, fifteen hours out from the drop point, that night I found her floating in my sleeping plates. I suppose I could have sent her to her own room, I mean it was within the laws of physics, but I didn't. I acted like conversation was the last thing I'd be interested in. But so did Feather.

"And the next morning it was all business, and a frantic business it was. We came in in devious fashion, and got off behind the moon. *Boy George* went on alone, decelerating. Passed too close to an ARM base on Claim 226 that even Feather wasn't supposed to know about. Turned around and accelerated away in clear and obvious terror, heading off in the general direction of Hrooshpith—pithtcha—of another of those used-to-be-kzinti systems where they've never got the population records straightened out. No doubt the ARM is waiting for us there.

"And of course you missed the ride down . . . but my point is that nothing ever got *said.*

"Okay. This whole scheme was schemed by Feather, carried through by Feather. It—" I stared into the black night. "Oh." I really should have seen this earlier. Why did Feather need Carlos?

Through the ARM spy net Feather Filip had found a family of six Shashters ready to emigrate. Why not look for one or two? Where Carlos insisted on taking his children and Sharrol and me, another man might be more reasonable.

"She doesn't just want to be clear of Sol system. Doesn't just want to make babies. She wants *Carlos.* Carlos of the perfect genes. Hah! Carlos finally saw it. Maybe she told him. He must have let her know he didn't want children by an ARM schiz. Angry and randy, she took it out on me, and then. . . ."

Then?

With my eyes open to the dark, entranced, I remembered that final night. *Yellow lights sprinkled on a black ocean. Some are the wrong color; too bright, too blue. Avoid those. They're houses. Pick one far from the rest. Hover. Organic matter burns lamplighter yellow below the drive flame, then fades. I sink us in, an egg in an egg cup. Feather blasts the roof loose and we crawl out—*

We hadn't wanted to use artificial lights. When dawn gave us enough light, we inflated the boat. Feather and Carlos used the gravity lift to settle the icebox in the boat. They were arguing in whispers. I didn't want to hear that, I thought.

I turned off the 'doc's "Maintenance" sequence. A minute later Sharrol sat up, a flat phobe wakened suddenly on an alien world. Sniffed the air. Kissed me and let me lift her out, heavy in Fafnir's gravity. I set her on the sand. Her nerve seemed to be holding.

Feather had procured local clothing; I pushed the bundle into her arms.

Feather came toward me towing the gravity lift. She looked shapeless, with bulging pockets fore and aft. We slid the lift into place, and I pushed the 'doc toward Carlos and the boat. Feather called my name. I turned. BLAM. Agony and scrambled senses, but I saw Carlos leap for the boat, reflexes like a jackrabbit. My head hit the black sand.

Then?

"She wanted hostages. Our children, but *Carlos's* children. They're frozen, they won't give her any trouble. But me, why would she need me? Killing me lets Carlos know she means it. Maybe I told too many stories: Maybe she thinks I'm dangerous. Maybe— "

For an instant I saw just *how* superfluous I was, from Feather Filip's psychotic viewpoint. Feather wanted Carlos. Carlos wanted the children. Sharrol came with the children. Beowulf Shaeffer was along because he was with Sharrol. If Feather shot Beowulf, how much would Carlos mind? BLAM.

Presently I said, "She shot me to prove she would. But it looked to me like Carlos just ran. There weren't any weapons in the boat, we'd only just inflated it. All he could do was start it and go. That takes—" When I thought about it, it was actually a good move. He'd gotten away with himself and Tanya and Louis, with both hostages. Protect them now, negotiate later.

And he'd left Feather in a killing rage, with that horrible tube and one living target. I stopped talking to Sharrol then, because it seemed to me she must be dead.

No! "Feather had you. She *had* to have *you*." It could happen. It could. "What else can she threaten Carlos with? She has to keep you alive." I tried to believe it. "She certainly didn't kill you in the first minute. Somebody had to put me in the 'doc. Feather had no interest in doing that."

But she had no interest in letting Sharrol do that either. "Tanj dammit! Why did Feather let you put me in the 'doc? She even let you. . . ." What about the biomass reserve?

My damaged body must have needed some major restructuring. The biomass reserve had been feeding Sharrol, and doing incidental repairs on us all, for the entire three week trip. Healing me would take another . . . fifty kilograms? More? "She must have let you fill the biomass reserve with. . . ." Fish?

Feather showing Carlos how reasonable she could be . . . too reasonable. It felt wrong, wrong. "The other body, the headless one. Why not just push *that* in the hopper? So much easier. Unless—"

Unless material was even closer to hand.

I felt no sudden inspiration. It was a matter of making myself believe. I tried to remember Sharrol . . . pulling her clothes on quickly, shivering and dancing on the sand, in the chilly dawn breeze. Hands brushing back through her hair, hair half grown out. A tiny grimace for the way the survival jacket made her look, bulges everywhere. Patting pockets, opening some of them.

The 'doc had snapped her out of a three-week sleep. Like me: awake, alert, ready.

It didn't go away, the answer. It just . . . I still didn't know where Sharrol was, or Carlos, or the children. What if I was wrong? Feather had mapped my route to Home, every step of the way. I knew exactly where Feather was now, if a line of logic could point my way. But—one wrong assumption, and Feather Filip could pop up behind my ear.

I could make myself safer, and Sharrol too, if I mapped out a worst-case scenario.

Feather's Plan B: Kill Shaeffer. Take the rest prisoners, to impose her will on Carlos ... but Carlos flees with the boat. So, Plan B-1: Feather holds Sharrol at gunpoint. (Alive.) Some days later she waves down a boat. BLAM, and a stolen boat sails toward Shasht. Or stops to stow Sharrol somewhere, maybe on another coral island, maybe prisoned inside a plastic tent with a live lamplighter horde prowling outside.

And Carlos? He's had four months, now, to find Sharrol and Feather. He's a genius, ask anyone. And Feather wants to get in touch ... unless she's given up on Carlos, decided to kill him.

If I could trace Carlos's path, I would find Louis and Tanya. I might even find Sharrol.

Carlos's Plan B-1 follows Plan A as originally conceived by Feather. The kids would be stowed aboard the iceliner as if already registered. Carlos would register and be frozen. Feather could follow him to Home ... maybe on the same ship, if she hustled. But—

No way could Feather get herself frozen with a gun in her hand. That would be the moment to take her, coming out of freeze on Home.

There, I had a target. On Shasht they could tell me who had boarded the *Zombie Queen* for Home. What did I have to do to get to Shasht?

"Feed myself, that's easy. Collect rainwater too. Get off the island...." That, at least, was not a puzzle. I couldn't build a raft. I couldn't swim to another island. But a sailor lost at sea will die if cast ashore; therefore local tradition decrees that he must be rescued.

"Collect some money. Get to Shasht. Hide myself." Whatever else was lost to me, to *us*—whoever had died, whoever still lived—there was still the mission, and that was to be free of the United Nations and Earth.

And Carlos Wu's 'doc was advanced nanotechnology: It screamed its Earthly origin. It might be the most valuable item on Fafnir, and I had no wealth at all, and I was going to have to abandon it.

Come daylight, I moved the 'doc. I still wanted to hide it in the lamplighter nest. The gravity lift would lift it but not push it uphill. But I solved it.

One of the secrets of life: Know when and what to give up.

I waited for low tide and then pushed it out to sea, and turned off the lift. The water came almost to the faceplate. Seven hours later it didn't show at all. And the next emergency might kill me unless it happened at low tide.

The nights were as warm as the days. As the tourist material had promised, it rained just before dawn. I set up my pants to funnel rainwater into a hole I chopped in the coral.

The tour guide had told me how to feed myself. It isn't that rare for a lamplighter nest to die. Sooner or later an unlit island will be discovered by any of several species of swimming things. Some ride the waves at night and spawn in the sand.

I spent the second night running through the shallows and scooping sunbunnies up in my jacket. Bigger flying fish came gliding off the crests of the breakers. They wanted the sun-bunnies. Three or four wanted me, but I was able to dodge. One I had to gut in midair.

The tour guide hadn't told me how to clean sunbunnies. I had to fake that. I poached them in seawater, using my pocket torch on high; I ate until I was bloated. I fed more of them into the biomass reservoir.

With some distaste, I fed those long human bones in too. Fafnir fish meat was deficient in metals. Ultimately that might kill me, but the 'doc could compensate for a time.

There was nothing to build a boat with. The burnt-out lamplighter nest didn't show by daylight, so any passing boat would be afraid to rescue me. I thought of swimming; I thought of riding away on the gravity lift, wherever the wind might carry me. But I couldn't feed myself at sea, and how could I approach another island?

On the fourth evening a great winged shape passed over the island, then dived into the sea. Later I heard a slapping sound as that flyer and a companion kicked themselves free of the water, soared, passed over the crater and settled into it. They made a great deal of noise. Presently the big one glided down to the water and was gone.

At dawn I fed myself again, on the clutch of eggs that had been laid in the body of the smaller flyer: male or female, whichever. The dime disk hadn't told me about this creature. A pity I wouldn't have the chance to write it up.

At just past sunset on the eighth night I saw a light flicker blue-green-red.

My mag specs showed a boat that wasn't moving.

I fired a flare straight up, and watched it burn blue-white

for twenty minutes. I fired another at midnight. Then I stuffed my boots partway into my biggest pockets, inflated my shoulder floats, and walked into the sea until I had to swim.

I couldn't see the boat with my eyes this close to water level. I fired another flare before dawn. One of those had to catch someone awake . . . and if not, I had three more. I kept swimming.

It was peaceful as a dream. Fafnir's ecology is very old, evolved on a placid world not prone to drifting continents and ice ages, where earthquakes and volcanoes know their place.

The sea had teeth, of course, but the carnivores were specialized; they knew the sounds of their prey. There were a few terrifying exceptions. Reason and logic weren't enough to wash out those memories, holograms of creatures the match for any white shark.

I grew tired fast. The air felt warm enough, the water did too, but it was leaching the heat from my flesh and bones. I kept swimming.

A rescuer should have no way of knowing that I had been on an island. The further I could get, the better. I did not want a rescuer to find Carlos Wu's 'doc.

❂

At first I saw nothing more of the boat than the great white wings of its sails. I set the pocket torch on wide focus and high power, to compete with what was now broad daylight, and poured vivid green light on the sails.

And I waited for it to turn toward me, but for a long time it didn't. It came in a zigzag motion, aimed by the wind, never straight at me. It took forever to pull alongside.

A woman with fluffy golden hair studied me in some curiosity, then stripped in two quick motions and dived in.

I was numb with cold, hardly capable of wiggling a finger. This was the worst moment, and I couldn't muster strength to appreciate it. I passively let the woman noose me under the armpits, watched the man lift me aboard, utterly unable to protect myself.

Feather could have killed me before the 'doc released me. Why wait? I'd worked out what must have happened to her; it was almost plausible, but I couldn't shake the notion that Feather was waiting above me, watching me come aboard.

There was only a brawny golden man with slanted brown eyes and golden hair bleached nearly as white as mine. *Tor*, she'd called him, and she was *Wil*. He wrapped me in a silver bubble blanket and pushed a bulb of something hot into my hands.

My hands shook. A cup would have splashed everything out. I got the bulb to my lips and sucked. Strange taste, augmented with a splash of rum. The warmth went to the core of me like life itself.

The woman climbed up, dripping. She had eyes like his, a golden tan like his. He handed her a bulb. They looked me over amiably. I tried to say something; my teeth turned into castanets. I sucked and listened to them arguing over who and what I might be, and what could have torn up my jacket that way.

When I had my teeth under some kind of control, I said, "I'm Persial January Hebert, and I'm eternally in your debt."

✻

Leaving all our Earthly wealth behind us was a pain. Feather could help: She contrived to divert a stream of ARM funds to Fafnir, replacing it from Carlos's wealth.

Riiight. But Sharrol and I would be sponging off Carlos ... and maybe it wouldn't be Carlos. Feather controlled that wealth for now, and Feather liked control. She had not said that she expected to keep some for herself. That bothered me. It must have bothered Carlos too, though we never found privacy to talk about it.

I wondered how Carlos would work it. Had he known Feather Filip before he reached Jinx? I could picture him designing something that would be useless on Earth: say, an upgraded version of the mass driver system that runs through the vacuum across Jinx's East Pole, replacing a more normal world's Pinwheel launcher. Design something, copyright it on Jinx under a pseudonym, form a company. Just in case he ever found the means to flee Sol system.

Me, I went to my oldest friend on Earth. General Products owed Elephant a considerable sum, and Elephant—Gregory Pelton—owed me. He got General Products to arrange for credit on Home and Fafnir. Feather wouldn't have approved the breach in secrecy, but the aliens who run General Products don't reveal secrets. We'd never even located their home world.

And Feather must have expected to control Carlos's funding and Carlos with it.

And Sharrol ... was with me.

She'd trusted me. Now she was a flat phobe broke and stranded on an alien world, if she still lived, if she wasn't the prisoner of a homicidal maniac. Four months, going on five. Long enough to drive her crazy, I thought.

How could I hurry to her rescue? The word hurry was said to be forgotten on Fafnir; but perhaps I'd thought of a way.

They let me sleep. When I woke there was soup. I was ravenous. We talked while we ate.

The boat was *Gullfish*. The owners were Wil and Tor, brother and sister, both recently separated from mates and enjoying a certain freedom. Clean air, exercise, celibacy, before they returned to the mating dance, its embarrassments and frustrations and rewards.

There was a curious turn to their accents. I tagged it as Australian at first, then as Plateau softened by speech training, or by a generation or two in other company. This was said to be typical of Fafnir. There was no Fafnir accent. The planet had been settled too recently and from too many directions.

Wil finished her soup, went to a locker, and came back with a jacket. It was not quite like mine, and new, untouched. They helped me into it, and let me fish through the pockets of my own ragged garment before they tossed it in the locker.

They had given me my life. By Fafnir custom my response would be a gift expressing my value as perceived by myself... but Wil and Tor hadn't told me their full names. I hinted at this; they failed to understand. Hmm.

My dime disk hadn't spoken of this. It might be a new custom: the rescuer conceals data, so that an impoverished rescuee need not be embarrassed. He sends no life gift instead of a cheap one. But I was guessing. I couldn't follow the vibes yet.

As for my own history—

"I just gave up," I blurted. "It was so stupid. I hadn't—hadn't tried everything at all."

Tor said, "What kind of everything were you after?"

"I lost my wife four months ago. A rogue wave—you know how waves crossing can build into a mountain of water? It rolled our boat under. A trawler picked me up, the *Triton.*" A civil being must be able to name his rescuer. Surely there must be a boat named Triton? "There's no record of anyone finding Milcenta. I bought another boat and searched. It's been four months. I was doing more drinking than looking lately, and three nights ago something rammed the boat. A torpedo ray, I think. I didn't sink, but my power was out, even my lights. I got tired of it all and just started swimming."

They looked at each other, then at their soup. Sympathy was there, with a trace of contempt beneath.

"Middle of the night, I was cold as the sea bottom, and it crossed my mind that maybe Mil was rescued under another name. We aren't registered as a partnership. If Mil was in a coma, they'd check her retina prints—"

"Use our caller," Wil said.

I thanked them. "With your permission, I'll establish some credit too. I've run myself broke, but there's credit at Shasht."

They left me alone in the cabin.

✹

The caller was set into a well in the cabin table. It was a portable—just a projector plate and a few keys that would get me a display of virtual keys and a screen—but a sailor's portable, with a watertight case and several small cleats. I found the master program unfamiliar but user-friendly.

I set up a search program for Milcenta Adelaide Graynor, in any combination. Milcenta was Sharrol and Adelaide was Feather, as determined by their iceliner tickets and retina prints. Milcenta's name popped up at once.

I bellowed out of the hatch. "They saved her!" Wil and Tor bolted into the cabin to read over my shoulder.

Hand of Allah, a fishing boat. Milcenta but not Adelaide! Sharrol had been picked up alone. I'd been at least half right: She'd escaped from Feather. I realized I was crying.

"No life gift." That was the other side of it: If she sent a proper gift, the embarrassment of needing to be rescued at sea need never become public record. We'd drilled each other on such matters. "She must have been in bad shape."

"Yes, if she didn't call you," Wilhelmin said. "And she didn't go home either?"

I told Martin Graynor's story: "We sold our home. We were on one last cruise before boarding an iceliner. She could be anywhere by now, if she thought the wave killed me. I'll have to check."

I did something about money first. There was nothing aboard *Gullfish* that could read Persial January Hebert's retina prints, but I could at least establish that money was there.

I tried to summon passenger records from the iceliner *Zombie Queen*. This was disallowed. I showed disappointment and some impatience, but of course they wouldn't be shown to Hebert. They'd be opened to Martin Wallace Graynor.

⁂

They taught me to sail.

Gullfish was built for sails, not for people. The floors

weren't flat. Ropes lay all over every surface. The mast stood up right through the middle of the cabin. You didn't walk in, you climbed. There were no lift plates; you slept in an odd-shaped box small enough to let you brace yourself in storms.

I had to learn a peculiar slang, as if I were learning to fly a spacecraft, and for the same reason. If a sailor hears a yell, he has to know what is meant, instantly.

I was working hard and my body was adjusting to the shorter day. Sure I had insomnia, but nobody sleeps well on a small boat. The idea is to snap awake instantly, where any stimulus could mean trouble. The boat was giving my body time to adjust to Fafnir.

Once I passed a mirror, and froze. I barely knew myself.

That was all to the good. My skin was darkening and, despite sunblock, would darken further. But when we landed, my hair had been cut to Fafnir styles. It had grown during four months in the 'doc. The 'doc had "cured" my depilation treatment: I had a beard too. When we reached civilization I would be far too conspicuous: a pink-eyed, pale-skinned man with long, wild white hair.

My hosts hadn't said anything about my appearance. It was easy to guess what they'd thought. They'd found a neurotic who sailed in search of his dead wife until his love of life left him entirely.

I went to Tor in some embarrassment and asked if they had anything like a styler aboard.

They had scissors. Riiight. Wil tried to shape my hair, laughed at the result, and suggested I finish the job at Booty Island.

So I tried to forget the rest of the world and just sail. It was what Wil and Tor were doing. One day at a time. Islands and boats grew more common as we neared the Central Isles. Another day for Feather to forget me, or lose me. Another day of safety for Sharrol, if Feather followed me to her. I'd have to watch for that.

And peace would have been mine, but that my ragged vest was in a locker that wouldn't open to my fingerprints.

Wil and Tor talked about themselves, a little, but I still didn't know their identities. They slept in a locked cabin. I noticed also an absence. Wil was a lovely woman, not unlike Sharrol herself; but her demeanor and body language showed no sign that she considered herself female, or me male, let alone that she might welcome a pass.

It might mean anything, in an alien culture: that my hair style or shape of nose or skin color were distasteful, or I didn't know the local body language, or I lacked documentation for my gene pattern. But I wondered if they wanted no life gift, in any sense, from a man they might have to give to the police.

What would a police detective think of those holes? Why, he'd think some kinetic weapon had torn a hole through the occupant, killing him instantly, after which someone (the killer?) had stolen the vest for himself. And if Wil and Tor were thinking that way.... What I did at the caller, might it be saved automatically?

Now *there* was a notion.

I borrowed the caller again. I summoned the encyclopedia and set a search for a creature with boneless arms. There were several on Fafnir, all small. I sought data on the biggest, particularly those local to the North Coral Quadrant. There were stories . . . no hard evidence.

And another day passed, and I learned that I could cook

while a kitchen was rolling randomly.

At dinner that night Wil got to talking about Fafnir sea life. She'd worked at Pacifica, which I gathered was a kind of underwater zoo; had I ever heard of a Kdatlyno life form like a blind squid?

"No," I said. "Would the kzinti bring one here?"

"I wouldn't think so. The kzinti aren't surfers," Tor said, and we laughed.

Wil didn't. She said, "They meant it for the hunting jungle. On Kdat the damn things can come ashore and drag big animals back into the ocean. But they've pretty well died out around Shasht, and we never managed to get one for Pacifica."

"Well," I said, and hesitated, and, "I think I was attacked by something like that. But huge. And it wasn't around Shasht, it was where you picked me up."

"Jan, you should report it."

"Wil, I can't. I was fast asleep and half dead of cold, lost at sea at midnight. I woke up under water. Something was squeezing my chest and back. I got my knife out and slashed. Slashed something rubbery. It pulled apart. It pulled my *jacket* apart. If it had ripped the shoulder floats I'd still be down there. But I never saw a thing."

Thus are legends born.

Booty Island is several islands merged. I counted eight peaks coming in; there must have been more. We had been sailing for twelve days.

Buildings sat on each of the lamplighter nests. They looked

like government buildings or museums. No two were alike. Houses were scattered across the flatlands between. A mile or so of shopping center ran like a suspension bridge between two peaks. On Earth this would have been a park. Here, a center of civilization.

A line of transfer booths in the mall bore the familiar flickering Pelton logo. They were all big cargo booths, and old. I didn't instantly see the significance.

We stopped in a hotel and used a coin caller. The system read my retina prints: Persial January Hebert, sure enough. Wil and Tor waited while I moved some money, collected some cash and a transfer booth card, and registered for a room. I tried again for records of Milcenta Adelaide Graynor. Sharrol's rescue was still there. Nothing for Feather.

Wil said, "Jan, she may have been recovering from a head injury. See if she's tried to find you."

I couldn't be Mart Graynor while Wil and Tor were watching. The net registered no messages for Jan Hebert. Feather didn't know that name. Sharrol did, but Sharrol thought I was dead.

Or maybe she was crazy, incapacitated. With Tor and Wil watching I tried two worst cases.

First: executions. A public 'doc can cure most varieties of madness. Madness is curable, therefore voluntary. A capital crime committed during a period of madness has carried the death penalty for seven hundred years, on Earth and on every world I knew.

It was true on Fafnir too. But Sharrol had not been executed for any random homicide, and neither, worse luck, had Feather.

Next: There are still centers for the study of madness. The best known is on Jinx. On Earth there are several, plus one secret branch of the ARM. There was only one mental institution to serve all of Fafnir, and that seemed to be half empty. Neither Feather's nor Sharrol's retina prints showed on the records.

The third possibility would have to wait.

We all needed the hotel's styler, though I was worst off. The device left my hair long at the neck, and theirs too, a local style to protect against sunburn. I let it tame my beard without baring my face. The sun had had its way with me: I looked like an older man.

I took Wil and Tor to lunch. I found "gullfish" on the menu, and tried it. Like much of Fafnir sea life, it tasted like something that had almost managed to become red meat.

I worked some points casually into conversation, just checking. It was their last chance to probe me too, and I had to improvise details of a childhood in the North Sea. Tor found me plausible; Wil was harder to read. Nothing was said of a vest or a great sea monster. In their minds I was already gone.

I was Schroedinger's cat: I had murdered and not murdered the owner of a shredded vest.

At the caller in my room I established myself as Martin Wallace Graynor. That gave me access to my wives' autodoc records. A public 'doc will correct any of the chemical imbalances we lump under the term 'crazy,' but it also records such service.

Milcenta Graynor—Sharrol—had used a 'doc eight times

in four-plus months, starting a week after our disastrous landing. The record showed much improvement over that period, beginning at a startling adrenalin level, acid indigestion and some dangerous lesser symptoms. Eight times within the Central Islands ... none on Shasht.

If she'd never reached the mainland, then she'd never tried to reach Outbound Enterprises. Never tried to find Carlos, or Louis and Tanya.

Adelaide Graynor—Feather—had no 'doc record on this world. The most obvious conclusion was that wherever she was, she must be mad as a March hare.

Boats named *Gullfish* were everywhere on Fafnir. Fifty-one registries. Twenty-nine had sail. Ten of those would sleep four. I scanned for first names: no Wil, no Tor. Maybe *Gullfish* belonged to a parent, or to one of the departed spouses.

I'd learned a term for *Gullfish's* sail and mast configuration: *sloop rig*.

Every one of the ten candidates was a sloop rig!

Wait, now. Wil had worked at Pacifica?

I did some research. Pacifica wasn't just a zoo. It looked more like an underwater village, with listings for caterers, costume shops, subs, repair work, travel, hotels ... but Wil had worked with sea life. Might that give me a handle?

I couldn't see how.

It wasn't that I didn't have an answer; I just didn't like it. Wil and Tor *had* to hand my vest to the cops. When Persial January Hebert was reported rescued, I would send them a gift.

Feather didn't know my alternate name. But if she had access to the Fafnir police, she'd tanj sure recognize that vest!

❂

With the rest of the afternoon I bought survival gear: a back-purse, luggage, clothing.

On Earth I could have vanished behind a thousand shades of dyes. Here ... I settled for a double dose of tannin secretion, an underdose of sunblock, a darkened pair of mag specs, my height, a local beard and hairstyle.

Arming myself was a problem.

The disk hadn't spoken of weapons on Fafnir. My safest guess was that Fafnir was like Earth: They didn't put weapons in the hands of civilians. Handguns, rifles, martial arts training belong to the police.

The good news: Everyone on the islands carried knives. Those flying sharks that attacked me during the sunbunny run were one predator out of thousands.

Feather would arm herself somehow. She'd look through a sporting goods store, steal a hunting rifle ... nope, no hunting rifles. No large prey on Fafnir, unless in the kzinti jungle, or *underwater.*

There were listings for scuba stores. I found a stun gun with a big parabolic reflector, big enough to knock out a one-gulp, too big for a pocket. I took it home, with more diving gear for verisimilitude, and a little tool kit for repairing diving equipment. With that I removed the reflector.

Now I couldn't use it underwater; it would knock *me* out, because water conducts sound very well. But it would fit my pocket.

❂

I took my time over a sushi dinner, quite strange. Some time after sunset I stepped into a transfer booth, and stepped out into a brilliant dawn on Shasht.

Outbound Enterprises was open. I let a Ms. Machti take Martin Wallace Graynor's retina prints. "Your ticket is still good, Mr. Graynor," Ms. Machti said. "The service charge will be eight hundred stars. You're four months late!"

"I was shipwrecked," I told her. "Did my companions make it?"

Iceliner passengers are in no hurry. The ships keep prices down by launching when they're full. I learned that the *Zombie Queen* had departed a week after our landing, about as expected. I gave Ms. Machti the names. She set the phone system searching, and presently said, "Your husband and the children boarded and departed. Your wives' tickets are still outstanding."

"Both?"

"Yes." She did a double-take. "Oh, good heavens, they must think you're dead!"

"That's what I'm afraid of. At least, John and Tweena and Nathan would. They were revived in good shape?"

"Yes, of course. But the women, could they have waited for you?"

Stet: Carlos, Tanya, and Louis were all safe on Home and had left the spaceport under their own power. Feather and Sharrol—"Waited? But they'd have left a message."

She was still looking at her screen. "Not for you, Mr. Graynor, but Mr. *John* Graynor has recorded a message for Mrs. Graynor . . . for Mrs. Adelaide Graynor."

For Feather. "But nothing for Milcenta? But they *both*

stayed? How strange." Ms. Machti seemed the type of person who might wonder about other people's sexual arrangements. I wanted her curious, because this next question—"Can you show me what John had to say to Adelaide?"

She shook her head firmly. "I don't see how—"

"Now, John wouldn't have said anything someone else couldn't hear. You can watch it yourself—" Her head was still turning left, right, left. "In fact, you should. Then you can at least tell *me* if there's been, if, well. I have to know, don't I? If Milcenta's dead."

That stopped her. She nodded, barely, and tapped in the code to summon Carlos's message to Feather.

She read it all the way through. Her lip curled just a bit, but she showed only solemn pity when she turned the monitor to face me.

It was a posed scene. Carlos looked like a man hiding a sickness. The view behind him could have been a manor garden in England, a tamed wilderness. Tanya and Louis were playing in the distance, hide-and-seek in and out of some Earthly tree that dripped a cage of foliage. Alive. Ever since I first saw them frozen, I must have been thinking of them as dead.

Carlos looked earnestly out of the monitor screen. "Adelaide, you can see that the children and I arrived safely. I have an income. The plans we made together, half of us have carried out. Your own iceliner slots are still available.

"I know nothing of Mart. I hope you've heard from him, but he should never have gone sailing alone. I fear the worst.

"Addie, I can't pretend to understand how you've changed,

how Mil changed, or why. I can only hope you'll both change your mind and come back to me. But understand me, Addie: You are not welcome without Milcenta. Your claim on family funds is void without Milcenta. And whatever relationship we can shape from these ashes, I would prefer to leave the children out of it."

He had the money!

Carlos stood and walked a half-circle as he spoke. The camera followed him on automatic, and now it showed a huge, sprawling house of architectural coral, pink and slightly rounded everywhere. Carlos gestured. "I've waited. The house isn't finished because you and Milcenta will have your own tastes. But come soon.

"I've set credit with Outbound. Messages sent to Home by hyperwave will be charged to me. I'll get the service charges when you and Milcenta board. Call first. We can work this out."

The record began to repeat. I heard it through again, then turned the monitor around.

Ms. Machti asked, "You went sailing alone?"

She thought I'd tried to commit suicide after our wives changed parity and locked the men out: an implication Carlos had shaped with some skill. I made a brush-off gesture and said, "I've got to tell him I'm still alive."

"The credit he left doesn't apply—"

"I want to send a hyperwave message, my expense. Let's see . . . does Outbound Enterprises keep a camera around?"

"No."

"I'll fax it from the hotel. When's the next flight out?"

"At least two weeks, but we can suspend you any time."

I used a camera at the hotel. The first disk I made would go through Outbound Enterprises. "John, I'm all right. I was on a dead island eating fish for awhile." A slightly belligerent tone: "I haven't heard a word from Adelaide or Milcenta. I know Milcenta better than you do, and frankly, I believe they must have separated by now. Home looks like a new life, but I haven't given up on the old one. I'll let you know when I know myself."

So much for the ears of Ms. Machti.

Time lag had me suddenly wiped out. I floated between the sleeping plates . . . exhausted but awake. What should I put in a *real* message?

Carlos's tape was a wonderful lesson in communication. He wants to talk to Feather. The children are not to be put at risk. Beowulf is presumed dead, c'est la vie, Carlos will not seek vengeance. But he wants Sharrol alive. Feather is not to come to Home without Sharrol. Carlos can enforce any agreement. He hadn't said so because it's too obvious. A frozen Feather, arriving at Home unaccompanied, need never wake.

And he had the money! Not just his own funds, but the money Feather knew about, "family funds": He must have reached civilization ahead of her and somehow sequestered what Feather funneled through the ARM. If Feather was loose on Fafnir, then she was also broke. She owned nothing but the credit that would get her a hyperwave call to Home, or herself and Sharrol shipped frozen. Though Carlos didn't know it, even Sharrol had escaped.

Nearly five months. How was Feather living? Did she have a job? Something I could track? With her training she might be better off as a thief.

Yah! I tumbled out of the sleepfield and tapped out my needs in some haste. She hadn't been caught at any capital crime, but any jail on Shasht would record Adelaide Graynor's retina prints. The caller ran its search. . . .

Nothing.

Okay, *job.* Feather needed something that would allow her time to take care of a prisoner. She had to have that if she had Sharrol, or in case she recaptured Sharrol, or captured *Beowulf.*

So I looked through some job listings, but nothing suggested itself. I turned off the caller and hoped for sleep. Perhaps I dozed a little.

Sometime in the night I realized that I had nothing more to say to Carlos.

Even Sharrol's escape wasn't information unless she stayed loose. Feather was a trained ARM. I was a self-trained tourist; I couldn't possibly hunt her down. There was only one way to hunt Feather.

It was still black outside, and I was wide awake. The caller gave me a listing of all-night restaurants.

I ordered an elaborate breakfast, six kinds of fish eggs, gulper bacon, cappuccino. Five people at a table demanded I join them, so I did. They were fresh from the coral isles via dirigible, still timelagged, looking for new jokes. I tried to oblige. And somewhere in there I forgot all about missing ladies.

We broke up at dawn. I walked back to the hotel alone. I had sidetracked my mind, hoping it would come up with something if I left it alone; but my answer hadn't changed. The way to hunt Feather was to pretend to be Feather, and hunt Sharrol.

Stet, I'm Feather Filip. What do I know about Sharrol? Feather must have researched her; she sure as tanj had researched me!

Back up. How did Sharrol get loose?

The simplest possible answer was that Sharrol dove into the water and swam away. Feather could beat her at most things, but a woman who lived beneath the ocean for thirty years could swim just fine.

Eventually a boat would find her.

Eventually, an island. Penniless. She needs work *now.* What kind of work is that? It has to suit a flat phobe. She's being hunted by a murderer, and the alien planet around her forces itself into her awareness every second. Dirigible stewardess is probably out. Hotel work would be better.

Feather, days behind her, seeks work for herself; but the listings will tell her Sharrol's choices too. And now I was back in the room and scanning through work listings.

Qualifications. I couldn't remember what Milcenta Graynor was supposed to be able to *do.* Sharrol's skills wouldn't match anyway, any more than mine matched Mart Graynor's. So look for *unskilled.*

Low salaries, of course. Except here: *servant, kzinti embassy.* Was that a joke? No: Here was *museum maintenance, must work with kzinti.* Some of them had stayed with the embassy, or even become citizens. Could Sharrol handle that? She got along with strangers . . . even near-aliens, like me.

Fishing boats, period of training needed. Hotel work. Underwater porter work, unskilled labor in Pacifica.

Pacifica. Of course.

Briefly I considered putting in for the porter job. Sharrol and/or Feather must have done that, grabbed whatever was to be had ... but I told myself that Feather thought I had no money. She'd never look for me in Pacifica's second-best ... ah, *best* hotel.

The truth is, I prefer playing tourist.

I scanned price listings for hotels in Pacifica, called and negotiated for a room at the Pequod. Then I left Shasht in untraditional fashion, via oversized transfer booth, still in early morning.

It was night in Pacifica. I checked in, crawled between sleeping plates and zonked out, my timelagged body back on track.

I woke late, fully rested for the first time in days. There was a little round window next to my nose. I gazed out, floating half mesmerized, remembering the Great Barrier Reef outside Carlos Wu's apartment.

The strangeness and variety of Earth's sea life had stunned me then. But these oceans were older. Evolution had filled ecological niches not yet dreamed on Earth.

It was shady out there, under a wonderful variety of seaweed growths, like a forest in fog. Life was everywhere. Here a school of transparent bell jars, nearly invisible, opened and closed to jet themselves along. Quasi-terrestrial fish glowed as if alien graffiti had been scrawled across them in dayglo ink to identify them to potential mates. Predators hid in the green treetops: Torpedo shapes dived from cover and disappeared back into the foliage with prey wriggling in long jaws.

A boneless arm swept straight down from a floating seaweed island, toward the orange neon fish swimming just above the sandy bottom. Its stinger-armed hand flexed and fell like a net over its wriggling prey ... and a great mouth flexed wider and closed over the wrist. The killer was dark and massive, shaped like a ray of Earth's sea. The smaller fish was painted on its back; it moved with the motion of the ray. The ray chewed, reeling the arm in, until a one-armed black oyster was ripped out of the seaweed-tree and pulled down to death.

One big beast, like a long dolphin with gills and great round eyes, stopped to look me over. Owl rams were said to be no brighter than a good dog, but Fafnir scientists had been hard put to demonstrate that, and Fafnir fishers still didn't believe it.

I waved solemnly. It bowed . . . well, bobbed in place before it flicked away.

My gear was arrayed in a tidy row, with the stunner nearest my hand. I'd put the reflector back on. I could reach it in an instant. Your Honor, *of course* it's for scuba swimming. Why else would I be in possession of a device that can knock Feather Filip into a coma before she can blow a great bloody hole through my torso?

I didn't actually want to go scuba swimming.

Sharrol swam like a fish; she could be out there right now. Still, at a distance and underwater, would I know her? And Feather might know me, and Feather would certainly swim better than me, and I could hardly ignore Feather.

Sharrol had to be living underwater. It was the only way she could stay sane. Life beyond the glass was alien, stet, but the life of Earth's seas seems alien too. My slow wits hadn't seen that at first, but Feather's skills would solve *that* puzzle.

And Beowulf Shaeffer had to be underwater, to avoid sunlight. Feather could find me for the wrong reasons!

And the police of Fafnir, of whom I knew nothing at all, might well be studying me in bemused interest. *He's bought a weapon!*

But why, if he has the blaster that blew a hole through this vest? And it's a fishing weapon, and he's gone to Pacifica ... which might cause them to hold off a few hours longer.

So, with time breathing hot on my neck, I found the hotel restaurant and took my time over fruit, fish eggs in a baked potato, and cappuccino.

My time wasn't wasted. The window overlooked a main street of Pacifica's village-sized collection of bubbles. I saw swimsuits, and casually dressed people carrying diving or fishing gear. Almost nobody dressed formally. That would be for Shasht, for going to work. In the breakfast room itself I saw four business tunics in a crowd of a hundred. And two men in dark blue police uniforms that left arms and legs bare: You could swim in them.

And one long table, empty, with huge chairs widely spaced. I wondered how often kzinti came in. It was hard to believe they'd be numerous, two hundred years after mankind took over.

Back in the room, I fished out the little repair kit and set to work on my transfer booth card.

We learned this as kids. The idea is to make a bridge of superconductor wire across the central circuits. Transport companies charge citizens a quarterly fee to cover local jumps. The authorities don't get upset if you stay away from the borders of the card. The borders are area codes.

Well, it *looked* like the kind of card we'd used then. Fafnir's booth system served a small population that didn't use booths much. It could well be decades old, long due for replacement. So I'd try it.

I got into casuals. I rolled my wet suit around the rest of my scuba gear and stuffed the stunner into one end where I could grab it fast. Stuffed the bundle into my backpurse—it stuck way out—and left the room.

Elevators led to the roof. Admissions was here, and a line of the big transfer booths, and a transparent roof with an awesome view up into the sea forest. I stepped into a booth and inserted my card. The random walk began.

A shopping mall, high up above a central well. Booths in a line, just inside a big water lock. A restaurant; another; an apartment building. I was jumping every second and a half.

Nobody noticed me flicking in; would they notice how quickly I flicked out? Nobody gets upset at a random walk unless the kids do it often enough to tie up circuits. But they might remember an adult. How long before someone called the police?

A dozen kzinti, lying about in cool half-darkness gnawing oddly shaped bones, rolled to a defensive four-footed crouch at the sight of me. I couldn't help it: I threw myself against the back wall. I must have looked crazed with terror when the random walk popped me into a Solarico Omni center. I was trying to straighten my face when the jump came. *Hey!* A travel terminal of some kind; I turned and saw the dirigible, like an underpressured planet, before the scene changed. *Her!*

Beyond a thick glass wall, the seaweed forest swarmed with

men and women wearing fins: farmers picking spheres that glowed softly in oil-slick colors. I waited my moment and snatched my card out of the slot. *Was it really* . . . I tapped quickly to get an instant billing, counted two back along the booth numbers. I couldn't use the jimmied card for this, so I'd picked up a handful of coins. . . . *Her?*

Solarico Omni, top floor. I stepped out of the booth, and saw the gates that would stop a shoplifter, and a stack of lockers.

For the first time I had second thoughts about the way I was dressed. Nothing wrong with the clothes, but I couldn't carry a mucking great package of diving gear into a shopping center, with a stunner so handy. I pushed my backpurse into a locker and stepped through the gates.

The whole complex was visible from the rim of the central well. It was darker down there than I was used to. Pacifica citizens must like their underwater gloom, I thought.

Two floors down, an open fast-food center: Wasn't that where I'd seen her? She was gone now. I'd seen only a face, and I could have been wrong. At least she'd never spot *me*, not before I was much closer.

But where was she? Dressed how? Employee or customer? It was midmorning: She couldn't be on lunch break. Customer, then. Only, Shashters kept poor track of time.

Three floors down, the Sports Department. Good enough. I rode down the escalator. I'd buy a spear gun or another stunner, shove everything into the bag that came with it. Then I could start window shopping for faces.

The Sports Department aisles were pleasantly wide. Most of what it sold was fishing gear, a daunting variety. There was skiing equipment too. And hunting, it looked like: huge weapons built for hands bigger than a baseball mitt. The smallest was a fat tube as long as my forearm, with a grip no bigger than a kzinti kitten's hand. Oh, sure, kzinti just love going to humans for their weapons.

Maybe the display was there to entertain human customers.

The clerks were leaving me alone to browse. Customs differ. *What the tanj was that?*

Two kzinti in the aisle, spaced three yards apart, hissing the Hero's Tongue at each other. A handful of human customers watched in some amusement. There didn't seem to be danger there. One wore what might be a loose dark blue swimsuit with a hole for the tail. The other (sleeveless brown tunic) took down four yards of disassembled fishing rod. A kzinti *clerk?*

The corner of my eye caught a clerk's hands (human) opening the case and reaching in for that smaller tube, with a grip built for a kzin child. Or a man.

My breath froze in my throat. I was looking into Feather's horrible ARM weapon. I looked up into the clerk's face.

It came out as a whisper. "No, Sharrol, no no no. It's me. It's Beowulf."

She didn't fire. But she was pale with terror, her jaw set like rock, and the black tube looked at the bridge of my nose.

I eased two inches to the right, very slowly, to put myself between the tube and the kzin cop. That wasn't a swimsuit he was wearing: It was the same sleeveless, legless police uniform I'd seen at breakfast.

We were eye to eye. The whites showed wide around her irises. I said, "My face. Look at my face. Under the beard. It's Bey, love. I'm a foot shorter. Remember?"

She remembered. It terrified her.

"I wouldn't fit. The cavity was built for Carlos. My heart and lungs were shredded, my back was shattered, my brain was dying, and you had to get me into the cavity. But I wouldn't fit, remember? Sharrol, I have to know." I looked around quick. An aisle over, kzinti noses came up, smelling fear. "Did you kill Feather?"

"Kill Feather." She set the tube down carefully on the display case. Her brow wrinkled. "I was going through my pockets. It was distracting me, keeping me sane. I needed that. The light was wrong, the gravity was wrong, the Earth was so far away—"

"Shh."

"Survival gear, always know what you have, *you* taught me that." She began to tremble. "I heard a sonic boom. I looked up just as you were blown backward. I thought I must be c-crazy. I couldn't have seen that."

It was my back that felt vulnerable now. I felt all those floors behind and above me, all those eyes. The kzin cop had lost interest. If there was a moment for Feather Filip to take us both, this was it.

But the ARM weapon was in *Sharrol's* hands. . . .

"But Carlos jumped into the boat and roared off, and Feather screamed at him, and you were all blood and sprawled out like—like dead—and I, I can't remember."

"Yes, dear," I took her hand, greatly daring, "but I have to know if she's still chasing us."

She shook her head violently. "I jumped on her back and cut her throat. She tried to point that tube at me. I held her arm down, she elbowed me in the ribs, I hung on, she fell down. I cut her head off. But Bey, there you were, and Carlos was gone and the kids were too, and what was I going to *do?*" She came around the counter and put her arms around me and said, "We're the same height. Futz!"

I was starting to relax. Feather was nowhere. We were free of her. "I kept telling myself you *must* have killed her. A trained ARM psychotic, but she didn't take you seriously. She couldn't have guessed how quick you'd wake up."

"I fed her into the organics reservoir."

"Yah. There was nowhere else all that biomass could have come from. It had to be Feather—"

"And I couldn't lift your body, and you wouldn't fit anyway. I had to cut off your h-h-" She pulled close and tried to push her head under my jaw, but I wasn't tall enough any more. "Head. I cut as low as I could. Tanj, we're the same *height.* Did it work? Are you all right?"

"I'm fine. I'm just short. The 'doc rebuilt me from my DNA, from the throat down, but it built me in Fafnir gravity. Good thing, too, I guess."

"Yah." She was trying to laugh, gripping my arms as if I might disappear. "There wouldn't have been room for your feet. Bey, we shouldn't be talking here. That kzin is a cop, and nobody knows how good their hearing is. Bey, I get off at sixteen hundred."

"I'll shop. We're both overdue on life gifts."

❂

"How do I look? How *should* I look?"

I had posed us on the roof of the Pequod, with the camera looking upward past us into the green seaweed forest. I said, "Just right. Pretty, cheerful, the kind of woman a man might drown himself for. A little bewildered. You didn't contact me because you got a blow to the head. You're only just healing. You ready? Take one, *now.*" I keyed the vidcamera.

Me: "Wilhelmin, Toranaga, I hope you're feeling as good as we are. I had no trouble finding Milcenta once I got my head on straight—"

Sharrol, bubbling: "Hello! Thank you for Jan's life, and thank you for teaching him to sail. I never could show him how to do that. We're going to buy a boat as soon as we can afford it."

Me: "I'm ready to face the human race again. I hope you are too. This may help." I turned the camera off.

"What are you giving them?" Sharrol asked.

"Silverware, service for a dozen. Now they'll *have* to develop a social life."

"Do you think they turned you in?"

"They had to. They did well by me, love. What bothers me is, they'll *never* be sure I'm not a murderer. Neither will the police. This is a wonderful planet for getting rid of a corpse. I'll be looking over my shoulder for that kzinti cop—"

"No, Bey—"

"He smelled our fear."

"They smell *everyone's* fear. They make wonderful police, but they can't react every time a kzin makes a human nervous. He may have pegged you as an outworlder, though."

"Oop. Why?"

"Bey, the kzinti are everywhere on Fafnir, mostly on the mainland, but they're on site at the fishing sources too. Fafnir sea life feeds the whole Patriarchy, and it's strictly a kzinti operation. Shashters are used to kzin. But kids and wimps and outworlders all get twitchy around them, and they're used to that."

He might have smelled more than our fear, I thought. Our genetic makeup, our diet ... but we'd been eating Fafnir fish for over a month, and Fafnir's people were every breed of man.

"Stet. Shall we deal with the *Hand of Allah?*"

Now she looked nervous. "I must have driven them half crazy. And worried them sick. It's a good gift, isn't it? Shorfy and Isfahan were constantly complaining about fish, fish, fish."

"They'll love it. It's about five ounces of red meat per crewman. I suppose that's—"

"Free range life forms from the hunting parks."

"—and fresh vegetables to match. I bet the kzinti don't grow *those*. Okay, take *one*."

Sharrol: "Captain Muh'mad, I was a long time recovering my memory. I expect the 'docs did more repair work every time I went under. My husband's found me, we both have jobs, and this is to entertain you and your crew in my absence."

Me: "For my wife's life, blessings and thanks." I turned it off. "Now Carlos."

Her hand stopped me. "I can't leave, you know," Sharrol said. "I'm not a coward—"

"Feather learned that!"

"It's just ... overkill. I've been through too much."

"It's all right. Carlos has Louis and Tanya for awhile, and that's fine, they love him. We're free of the UN. Everything went just as we planned it, more or less, except from Feather's viewpoint."

"Do you mind? Do you like it here?"

"There are transfer booths if I want to go anywhere. Sharrol, I was raised underground. It feels just like home if I don't look out a window. I wouldn't mind spending the rest of our lives here. Now, this is for Ms. Machti at Outbound, not to mention any watching ARMs. Ready? Take *one.*"

Me: "Hi, John! Hello, kids! We've got a more or less happy ending here, brought to you with some effort."

Sharrol: "I'm pregnant. It happened yesterday morning. That's why we waited to call."

I was calling as Martin Wallace Graynor. Carlos/John could reach us the same way. We wanted no connection between Mart Graynor and Jan Hebert.

Visuals were important to the message. The undersea forest was behind us. I stood next to Sharrol, our eyes exactly level. That'd give him a jolt.

Me: "John, I know you were worried about Mil, and so was I, but she's recovered. Mil's a lot tougher than even Addie gave her credit for."

Sharrol: "Still, the situation was sticky at first. Messy." She rubbed her hands. "But that's all over. Bey's got a job working outside in the water orchards—"

Me: "It's just like working in free fall. I've got a real knack for it."

Sharrol: "We've got some money too, and after the baby's born I'll take Bey's job. It'll be just like I'm back in my teens."

Me: "You did the right thing, protecting the children first. It's worked out very well."

Sharrol: "We're happy here, John. This is a good place to raise a child, or several. Some day we'll come to you, I think, but not now. The changes in my life are too new. I couldn't take it. Mart is willing to indulge me."

Me: [sorrowfully] "Addie is gone, John. We never expect to see her again, and we're just as glad, but I feel she'll always be a part of me." I waved the camera off.

Now let's see Carlos figure *that* out. He does like puzzles.

WHERE NEXT, COLUMBUS?

WITH JERRY POURNELLE

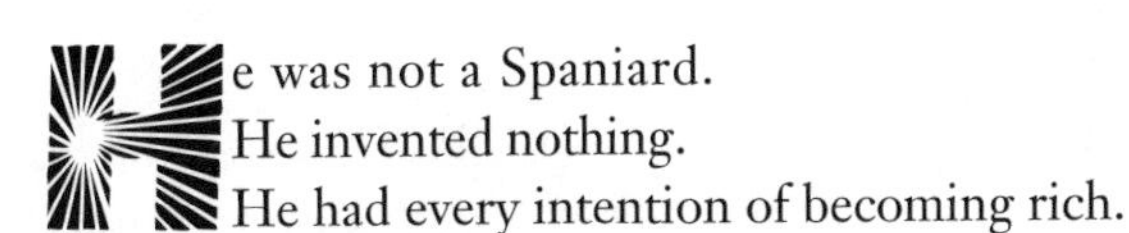

He was not a Spaniard.

He invented nothing.

He had every intention of becoming rich.

You've known these things since grade school; but you may well have missed the point. So let's try again.

Christopher Columbus was not a Spaniard. Precisely what he was isn't clearly agreed. Some say he was the son of a Genoese weaver, others say he was the scion of a family of converted Jews. His own biography, written by his son, claims his kinship to the Count Colombo of Montferrat, but few believe that. It is more likely that his father was Domenico Colombo, weaver and owner of a wineshop in Genoa; it is certain that he was a Genoese citizen, since we have transcripts of his evidence as a witness in a trial there.

He became a merchant seaman, then merchant adventurer, and whatever his ancestry he had enough ability to move into ever higher society. Eventually he traveled to Portugal and married there the daughter of the Governor of Porto Santo, the companion island of Madeira, so that he could claim Portuguese citizenship if he wanted it. He was introduced to the

King of Portugal, and proposed to him a voyage of exploration. Those negotiations came to nothing, and he moved to Spain, where he made the same proposals.

These were his demands: that he was to be Grand Admiral of the Oceanic Sea, Viceroy for life of all lands he discovered; that he would collect ten percent of the whole commerce of any lands he discovered. This was an enormous price, and he stuck to it through all. He insisted on his price and perquisites even when that was all that stood between him and his expedition. This was what he proposed to the Portuguese, then to the Spanish, and he would not haggle or compromise. He would risk all that was his, he would risk ridicule, discomfort and death, but he wanted the fruits of his labor.

He was no innovator. Despite the legends, anyone worth talking to knew that the world was round, and most knew its size. In 1481 Pope Pius II himself observed that nearly everyone was then agreed that the world was round.

Columbus had a vision of wealth and commerce flowing from an expedition to "India" or the Japans. So did others; in fact, nearly everyone who thought about the situation knew there was a vast potential for riches if a new way to the Orient could be found, and quite a few merchant adventurers were convinced a ship could sail around the world.

Somebody else's ship. Let someone else take the risks.

The analogy with the modern world is striking. Five hundred years since since the voyages of Columbus, the planet has changed almost beyond recognition; but Columbus's time has come round again.

First, most planetary scientists understand that there is vast wealth in the solar system; that ninety percent of the resources easily available to mankind are not on the earth at all. Space is a potential source of both minerals and energy dwarfing all others: a new world indeed, and one that's fairly easy to get to if we build the right tools of access.

It's hardly a secret. It's just that no one quite wants to be next to go there. We've landed men on the Moon, and planted a flag. Unfortunately, we didn't really claim the territory, and we haven't settled on it, and we haven't exploited it, and we haven't provided access to it. Going there was a stunt. Once it was done, it was thought that it didn't need to be done again; but everyone knows how to do it.

Second, the United States seems determined that no one will get rich from space exploration. Robert Heinlein's "The Man Who Sold The Moon" tells of an entrepreneur who risks everything to open the routes to the Moon. Heinlein's Delos D. Harriman, already rich, risks everything he owns; he expects to get richer, and to make a number of others rich in the bargain. In the story he has the hidden motive of being in love with space itself, of being not the hard-hearted businessman he appears to be, but a dreamer. Still, he hides that well. To the world he looks to gain more wealth from exploiting the Moon.

In real life, no one has made a nickel from the Moon.

The Apollo program was terribly expensive, and every dime of the money was spent on Earth. Of course some companies got rich, but they made their money from building the ships, not from commerce. It's as if the only profits to be made from Columbus's expeditions went to the Brothers Pinzon at Palos, who built the *Nina*, the *Pinta*, and the *Santa Maria*.

There's more to the story. Martin Alonzo Pinzon planned a westward voyage of discovery before he ever met Columbus, and he and his family financed Columbus's final and successful trip to the Court of Ferdinand and Isabella the Great. Columbus was no navigator; he never did learn to use the sextant or calculate a latitude. Indeed, his reputation as a shipmaster was so bad that no sailors would join his expedition until the Pinzons were brought in.

Yet Columbus was needed. The Pinzons had never been able to persuade the Spanish Court to grant them the concessions and titles that would allow them to become rich from the voyage. Columbus's trick wasn't to sail west—others thought of that, and had the means to do it. What Columbus managed was to get the Court to grant him his titles and tithes: to give him the means of enriching himself from the commerce that would follow a successful voyage.

Isabella pledging the Crown Jewels to finance the taming of a new world. What a concept! As if we could finance a lunar base by imposing a tax upon each member of Congress! At least they would then have some interest in building a cheap, effective space program—

But even Columbus couldn't manage that.

The Spanish Court contributed some money for his expedition, but that wasn't decisive. Despite the myth, the amounts actually advanced were fairly modest: a one-time payment of less than one and a half million maravedis, or under two percent of the annual Spanish budget. The United States spent more in proportion to our annual budget on Apollo, and more again on NASA's incredible shrinking paper space station.

What was decisive was the titles and concessions: Columbus, and his private backers the Pinzons, were assured that if they were successful they'd get rich. The Spanish Government pledged that it wouldn't simply confiscate the rewards of success. There was no "Moon Treaty" to confiscate the resources of the universe for some mythical common heritage of mankind. Columbus would keep what he earned.

Finally, Columbus wasn't a Spaniard. Provided that he would be allowed to keep the spoils of his success, he'd have been willing to sail for his native Genoa; for his wife's Portugal; for Spain; or, as a last resort, for Genoa's archenemy Venice. He didn't have an introduction to the English Court or he'd probably have tried that. He certainly faked negotiations with the French—indeed, a feigned visit to the King of France was the decisive event in causing Isabella to order the Court to give Columbus the contract he demanded.

If Columbus proposed a Mars Expedition to the US government today, what would happen? It's extremely unlikely that he'd be granted any concessions or monopolies. Our civilization no longer believes people ought to get rich.

The wealth of eternity is over our heads. The energy of an entire star. Metals from asteroids, chemical wealth from gas giant planets, titanium on the Moon. For years we've told these truths to ourselves and each other and anyone who will listen.

And they do listen! In this year 1992 AD, anyone worth

talking to has at least a vague notion that the wealth of Fantasyland is to be found in space. Test this for yourself. Ask a bright friend:

What killed the dinosaurs? (Giant meteoroid impact.)

How does anyone know? (High iridium content in the clay laid down at that time. It's vaporized asteroid. Meteoroids are rich in metals of the platinum family.

Iridium? That's valuable, isn't it? (Yeah.)

They know; why don't they care?

Because an entrepreneur must gamble everything. Because his best opportunity is to go broke. Because even if he wins his gamble, his winnings may go to the IRS, or some other government office, or some random lawyer.

❂

When the Gang of Eight Stooges collapsed in Moscow, nobody ever interviewed Ronald Reagan. Why not? Did he not have some hand in encouraging the decline of the USSR? Or is it perceived that Soviet communism collapsed of its own basic flaws?

Whatever. We have our own problems—

Ours is a capitalistic civilization. The Soviets used to remind us of that from time to time. Now the communist empire has collapsed. They'll try to learn capitalism, but who will they find for an example? Who will remind *us* that we're capitalists? Who will remember that the essence of capitalism is that big risky ventures let you go broke—or get rich.

You won't learn it in universities. The economy of a university runs very like the upper levels of the old Soviet Union: Dominance games are played for salaries and funding, and what is produced—educated students—is nearly irrelevant. There's nothing of capitalism in universities.

You won't learn it from NASA. When NASA had money and it looked as if there would be a lot of trouble-free shuttle flights, NASA had a favorite trick, a trick favored by our railroad barons of the late nineteenth century. Robber barons don't like competition; they would really prefer a monopoly. Whenever anyone tried to invest money in space activities, NASA would undercut their price, offering to provide the same service for less, using tax money. And NASA had become as powerful as a hydraulic empire. Their bureaucracies *cannot* be destroyed.

When you're in orbit you're halfway to anywhere.

You don't have a space program if you don't have a vehicle. The United States has no program to provide access to space for any but a handful of specialists. There is no way you or I or an average businessman could go to space.

Yet the price need not be so high. Access to space is possible, at costs comparable to the cost of first class transoceanic air flight. Space costs so much now because it is designed to cost so much. It need not.

There is in the United States a new breed of rocket ship designer. These are people who grew up around the old rocket industry, but also grew up knowing how to use small computers; who understand the new light-weight structural materials, and who have learned how to keep things simple.

These people have repeatedly proposed programs costing less than a billion dollars, to build spacecraft amenable to airline-style operations.

The ships they envision would fly to orbit, return to any of a scattering of cheaply built spaceports, and fly again without having to be gutted like a fish, receive new entrails by implant, then be covered anew in new scales. The SSX—Space Ship Experimental—program has been evaluated by dozens of expert committees, and no one really disagrees that spaceships that operate like airplanes can be built.

But to make it work, we need Columbus again, or D.D. Harriman. Mankind will not have begun the conquest of space until somebody has been *seen* to get rich *from space.*

Christopher Columbus was not a Spaniard, but he brought Spain a great empire of wealth and resources. The New Columbus may not be Japanese. . . .

THE COLOR OF SUNFIRE

My contract with the Pleione ended on Silvereyes.

Silvereyes was Earthlike, blue-on-blue under shredded white cloud. Earthlike, except for the sunflower fields. Every world, even every habitable world, has its own strange signature. The atmospheric bands and prolate shape of Jinx, the freeway lines girding Earth, the cue-ball white of Mount Lookitthat, and now, finally, the silver sunflower fields of Silvereyes, Beta Hydri I.

There were five such fields spaced around the planet. Five oval fields of sunflowers, each the approximate size of, say, Mongolia or Iran. If you caught the planet just right, with two of the fields showing in daylight, they looked like gleaming silver eyes peering into space. Clouds couldn't block that glare, could barely dim it. The eyes peered blindly up to watch us land.

Earth, Jinx, Wunderland, We Made It—for three years I had lived with the Pleione, hauling goods among the home worlds. Each time we went up we were richer. My contract was up, my money was banked, and I was down for good. I would be a landowner on Silvereyes, at least long enough to know whether I liked it.

The spaceport was at the edge of one of the huge sunflower fields. From the fence to the horizon the sunflowers grew, thick, knotted grey stalks two feet high, topped each by a rippling blossom with a silver mirror surface. Each towel-sized mirror blossom was turned toward the late afternoon sun, and each was curved into a paraboloid of rotation, its focus on a black photosynthetic knot protruding from the blossom.

Nothing lived in that field besides sunflowers. Any trespassing plant or animal would have been blasted for fertilizer, blasted to ash in the blinding focus of rippling solar mirrors.

I gawked at the sunflowers for awhile, thinking philosophical thoughts. Then, carrying my luck-gift, I walked to a transfer booth. I dropped a coin in the slot and dialed at random.

Tomorrow I would look for property to buy. Tonight I would celebrate.

Luck brought me out in a private residence somewhere in the world. A stick-thin householder unfolded himself from his masseur chair to stare inquiringly at me. I called, "What town is this?"

"Bradbury's Landing," said the worthy. "Do I know you?"

"Doubtful." I opened the door to place my luck-gift in a shelf outside the booth. It was a copy of a Hrodenu tough-sculpture, lacking something of the original no doubt, but a good piece, and expensive. "A luck-gift for the first silverman I was to meet. If you'll name me the best bar in town, I'll not disturb you further."

"Try Grushenko's," he said immediately. "But let me offer you a drink first. My name is Mann."

I would have refused. To take something in return might spoil the luck. But now I had a better look at him, and I knew he wasn't a silverman after all.

He was a Wunderlander. The asymmetric beard made it certain, though his attenuated seven foot frame showed his low gravity origin. He had the dignity to go with the beard, the straight posture, the unconscious air of nobility. A wonder it had lasted, for he must be desperately poor.

And poor men don't leave their own worlds. They can't afford to. Curious....

"Taken," I said. "And I'll trade you tales."

"A good custom," said Mann. "I followed it at one time." He dipped into a cupboard and brought out a bottle. "I'd offer you your choice, but there is only vodka. It's good in drooble-berry juice, or chilled and tossed back over the palate."

"Chilled then. I plan to be drunk before the night ends. Is it night here?"

"Barely." He seemed startled. "What did you do, dial at random?"

"Yes."

He laughed. He pulled out a worn low-temp container, opened it and dipped the bottle. The liquid inside boiled and smoked. Liquid nitrogen. He held the bottle until water started to freeze out of the vodka, then poured. He bowed as he handed me the drink.

I bowed and handed him the touch-sculpture copy, though the luck had gone out of the gesture. A pity I hadn't met a silverman.

"Call me Richard," he said. "Richard Harvey Schultz-Mann. And who shall tell his tale first?"

"Yourself," I said. I'd chosen my own tale, of a bander-snatch hunt near the Jinxian shoreline, and of the telepathic woman who needed a bandersnatch skeleton to complete her collection. But she kept fainting, with no apparent medical cause. She was an experienced huntress. Though she knew about bandersnatchi, her habit was to read the mind of her prey. Sensory deprivation kept putting her to sleep....

But what of his tale? He must be churchrat poor. I was not judging only by his small apartment nor by his aged clothing. He himself was aged. Half his beard and most of his hair were white. His withered skin look like he'd slept in it. A man who doesn't buy boosterspice is a man on the edge of starvation.

Richard Harvey Schultz-Mann tossed a jigger of vodka back over his palate. "Would you believe that I once had it in my power to blackmail the entire puppeteer species?"

"Certainly," I said. "You're my host."

"Meaning I could tell you anything at all." He laughed. "But this is true. Once I knew the location of the puppeteer home world. You may remember that that was the species' most closely guarded secret, before their exodus."

"I remember. They pulled up stakes about forty years ago." My family had gone broke in the crash. Half the interworld businesses in known space had folded for lack of the puppeteers. Once day their commercial empire had offices on every known habitable world. The next, they were gone, their commitments paid off in cash.

Rumors were rife. The most consistent was that the galactic core had exploded in a chain reaction of novae, and the puppeteers had found out about it. The radiation wave wouldn't be reaching known space for another twenty thousand years, which you'd say is a good long time. But the puppeteers were cowards. They had left, in the fastest species migration on record.

Luckily I'd already earned my spaceman's papers. With no money left, I'd have had to drop out of grad school.

Like the Jinxian, raiding their ships, or worse. An armed invasion, a hundred years from now, or a thousand, or ten thousand. You see?"

"Yah. He told you where their world was?"

"As he was dying," said Rich Mann. "Twenty-three point six, seventy point one, six point nil. That was what he said."

"Just one world, I assume."

"Of course. Not one puppeteer in a million would be brave enough or insane enough to trust itself in a fragile spacecraft. Each of their representatives to other worlds was more or less insane. How could they colonize other worlds? By sending maniacs?"

"I used to wonder why nobody ever found that world. It must be somewhere in known space, or not far outside. People must have looked. Newsmen, fortune hunters, hobbyists. Spacemen aren't known for a repressed curiosity."

"They didn't know what they were looking for." Mann lay back in a fading masseur chair whose machinery had long ceased working. Once I would have commented on the odd contours of his beard, covering his right cheek entirely, sprouting in a single waxed spike at the left point of his chin, shaved off entirely below the part in his hair. But I'd seen too many odd customs on too many odd worlds. I'd even found people to comment on my own customs, and to laugh at them.

"I found out," he said. "That was my mistake. I should have gone straight back to civilization, looked up the puppeteer embassy and made a deal. Memory erasure of those coordinates, for a fee of a hundred million stars. Right then, no hesitation. They'd have jumped at the chance.

"But I had to see for myself. What was it you said about spacemen and curiosity?

"I took my ship, my borrowed ship that was owned by the Institute of Knowledge on Jinx, and I went to twenty-three point six, seventy point one, six point nil. And what I found was a big, fat, fuzzy red giant. Talk about the purloined letter! Men must have been watching that star with telescopes before ever they flew."

"Naturally I believe you," I said. "Every word, immediately. But I seem to remember that the puppeteers walked in Earth's gravity, breathed terrestrial air, and never wore protective clothing against the ultraviolet waves in sunlight." Mann was grinning like he had my wallet. "All right, I know I'm off the track, but how? The puppeteers must have come from a nearly Earthlike world under a nearly GO sun."

"That's where everyone else went off the track, too. They were all searching around G- and F- class sun. Funny thing is, that fat red giant probably *was* a yellow dwarf a million or two years ago."

"But—"

"How about Procyon? We Made It has a population near a billion, yet everyone knows it'll start expanding in half a million years. We'll be gone long before then, of course. The Core explosion.

"I see why you're confused, of course. I saw that red giant, and I decided the Jinxian had lied to me after all. I searched what should have been the habitable temperature bands. I found rocks up to the size of Ceres, no bigger. I'd been assuming a transparent, Earthlike atmosphere. Now I searched further and further out, assuming denser atmosphere, more greenhouse effect. I searched out to two billion miles from the primary. Nothing. The Jinxian had lied."

Mann got up to refill our glasses. I said. "If that's your story, I'm going to brain you with a Hrodenu."

"It almost was the end. I was a week toward Silvereyes before I turned back.

"I'd been thinking. The puppeteers were used to G-type sunlight. If their world was actually circling a red giant sun, they must be using supplementary ultraviolet. That would release more heat on their world. Plants would need it too. More heat, higher temperatures. They'd be further out."

"You could carry that on forever," I speculated. "Assume more and more power per individual, more and more individuals. Any flatlander uses more power in a day than a citizen of Russia, at its peak of power, used in a lifetime. Seawater distilleries alone. . . ."

"Now you've got it," said Mann.

"Excuse me?"

"Think it out the way I did. The puppeteers are cowards. They couldn't relieve their population pressure by migration. So the population of the home world went up and up. So did the power expenditure per capita.

"It's the same on Earth. It never snows on the big cities, because the people are putting out too much power. Street lights, house lights—why, if a reading lamp put out only visible light, the only light that didn't get absorbed by the walls would be the fraction that escaped to space through windows. Then there are refrigerators, air conditioning, transfer booths, crematoriums, neon signs, the frequencies of tridee transmission, messages lasered in from the Moon and asteroids. How

A thought hit me. "Is that how you lost your money? In the puppeteer crash?"

He looked at me from under shaggy white brows. His eyes were black and deep. "Yes and no. I wasn't in the stock market. I was tracing relics of tnuctipun biological engineering, flying my ship on a government grant. I set my ship down on a world orbiting Mira Ceti, and there I met a Jinxian."

"You were tracing what?"

"Old plants, genetically tailored by the tnuctipun, left behind when the tnuctipun were wiped out. They've been mutating for more than a billion years. I was tracing stage trees, but those sunflowers outside are more of the same."

"Oh, really?"

"The Slavers used them for defense, surrounding their plantations with sunflower borders. The tnuctipun used them to attack the plantations. Afterward, the sunflowers throve. A built-in heat beam is more effective against predators than mere thorns.

"Then there are the air plants. Another tailored plant, once used to replace air on Slaver ships. Later they learned to hold their air in bubbles. Now they cover dozens of known asteroid belts. But I digress," said Mann.

I assured him I'd been fascinated. He smiled and refilled our glasses. I was sipping at my own vodka, for it was stinging cold. I'd have choked myself if I'd tried to drink it like he did.

"The Jinxian," he said, "had found the puppeteer system. He was making pirate raids on them. Idiot. He'd have been rich beyond dreams if he'd simply blackmailed them. They're cowards, the puppeteers. They were afraid that if men knew where their world was, someday they might try to rob them.

about underwater street lights in the continental shelf cities? And dolphin industries? It all has to go somewhere. And Earth's population is only eighteen billion."

"How many puppeteers are there?"

Mann shrugged, "I didn't get that close. A trillion, I'd guess, and all fanatics for comfort. They must use total conversion for power. Would you believe—"

"Instantly."

"You're kind. I found the puppeteer planet two light-weeks out from its primary. The sun was no more than a blurred pink dot."

I closed my mouth.

"I'll be damned," Mann said wonderingly. "You meant it. You haven't called me a liar yet. But it makes sense to put a planet out there. With all the heat they were putting out, they needed a sun like they needed an armed kzinti invasion. A long, long time ago they must have moved their world out to where they could radiate enough heat away to keep the planet habitable. When the sun blew up like a big red balloon, the chances are they hardly noticed."

"No wonder they were never found. Why do you suppose they kept a sun at all?"

"They probably wanted an anchor, to keep them from drifting all over space."

"Um."

"You should have seen it, the way it blazed against the stars. Not like a planet. The continents flamed like yellow-star sunlight. I could have read a book in the light that came through my windows."

"They let you get that close?"

"Who'd have dared attack me?" He was taking to himself now, and his thoughts were nowhere in this room. "The continents flamed like sunfire, but the oceans were black as space, with light scattered across them to mark islands, maybe. Points of light like bright stars. It was as if black, starry space pushed its edges through black, starry seas to the borders of the burning continents. I'm the only man alive who's ever seen it. The Jinxian saw it, he and his pirate crew, but they're dead. All dead."

"How do you know?"

"I killed them."

"Did you have reason?"

"Ample reason. Points of honor," said Mann. He knocked his vodka back with a flip of the wrist. "The Jinxian gave me the coordinates as he was dying. Revenge, he thought. He was right. I should have gone straight to We Made It, but I had to see the planet for myself. And then I came to Silvereyes, which was closer, and I went to the puppeteer embassy, and it was gone."

"Oh," I said, for I had the whole picture.

"That's right. While I was looking for their planet, the puppeteers found out about the Core explosion. So they fled the worlds of men, and where did that leave me? The Institute decided I'd misused my ship. Presently they confiscated it."

"Surely you could have gotten something out of it. You knew where the puppeteer world was."

"Did I?" He grinned mockingly.

"Sure. A news agency would have paid you plenty for the biggest scoop of the generation. Even if the puppeteers had left their world empty behind them."

"But they didn't."

"Excuse me?"

"They didn't have to travel in hyperspace, because they weren't coming back. The relativistic time lag wouldn't inconvenience them. They felt safer in normal space. That meant there was no limit to the mass they could move."

"Eventually, my host, you will strain even my credulity."

"Why boggle at this? They'd already moved their world once. They hated spacecraft. This is no random guess. When I couldn't find an embassy I decided to go straight to the puppeteers themselves. I left a message behind in a safe deposit box, to protect myself, like any blackmailer. The puppeteer world was gone when I got there. Gone like a dream. I turned back to Silvereyes, and there the Institute confiscated my ship. Ship and score and riches beyond dreams, all gone.

"Now I have only the memory of a world that shone by its own light, that blazed in the colors of sunfire and darkness." He hefted the Hrodenu. "And this. I thank you. Every man should own one good thing."

A pretty compliment. "It was well traded," I told him. "And the vodka is almost gone. Shall we go drinking and dining? You can play guide for me, since you've been here for forty years."

And so Mann donned clothing and we went to Grushenko's, I and the finest liar in known space. There, hours later, we traded tales with a pair of sloe-eyed computer programmers. One girl, by luck, turned out to have a father-fixation; and so we were well paired.

It was a fine night to be down. The only uncomfortable moment came when Mann retold his tale of the puppeteer world, and produced a pocket holograph. Somehow the luck of the gift held, and Mann didn't see my jaw drop.

There in the holograph, a light the color of the sun blazed against starry space. The blazing figure had the shape of a fiery amoeba, but two reaching pseudopods had been lopped at their tips by arcs of a circle.

"I wonder where it is now," said Mann. The beauty he saw in the holograph, the beauty I could not see, was all the beauty there is.

THE LÉSHY CIRCUIT

UNFINISHED SCRIPT FOR PLANETARIUM SHOW

Audience takes their seats. Auditorium darkens.

Scene one is detailed. We are looking out of Queen Moriah *(no part of the ship shows) at nearby spacecraft, shuttlecraft and Bussard ramjets. Beyond these are the more distant and far larger O'Neill colonies, with some variation in design; an older model is partly disassembled. Beyond these is a crescent of the planet Miramon Lluagor. The red dwarf Ross 614 drifts behind the planet during the introduction, causing an eclipse.*

Alternatively, we can start with the simple, cryptic diagram of the Léshy circuit, raise the color organ, then throw all this onscreen.

ANNOUNCER: The universe is big. The more you know, the bigger it gets. Even the gaps between the nearest stars are great enough to shrink a man to nothing. To cross such gaps seems impossible for tiny, short-lived human beings.

But men have crossed impossible gaps before now. The pioneers go half-expecting to lose their lives. Those who follow go in greater safety, with greater knowledge. Eventually the crossing becomes routine.

Can it be that a voyage between the stars will ever be . . . routine?

Raise color organ

Credits:

THE LÉSHY CIRCUIT
AN ORIGINAL STAR SHOW
WRITTEN FOR HANSEN PLANETARIUM BY
LARRY NIVEN

Voices are low volume at first.

JENNER: They're all aboard, Captain. All but two.

CAPTAIN: Oh?

JENNER: The shuttle jockey says two of 'em chickened out.

CAPTAIN: [*Laughs*] All right, Jenner. We ready? You haven't forgotten anything?

JENNER: [*Amused and offended*] You kidding? Do you know how many circuits I've made?

CAPTAIN: Two, and you will address me as "Ma'am."

JENNER: Yes ma'am.

CAPTAIN: Can you keep the passengers happy while I start the rams?

JENNER: Sure. [*His voice becomes louder as he addresses his audience directly.*] Welcome aboard the ramship *Queen Moriah*, one of the oldest Bussard ramjet starships still in service. There are seventy of you in each of three passenger compartments. You probably won't have time to get to know each other before we arrive in Procyon system, but go ahead and try if you like.

Something like a hundred and fifty of you arrived in Ross 614 system four days ago, aboard this ship. I hope and presume you enjoyed playing tourist among the Wheel Cities. If you've heard some of my speech before, please bear with me, because the others haven't.

For those of you who have just joined us, welcome! I'm a Lluagorian myself. My city of origin is New West Berlin—

A light pointer indicates a smaller wheel city of older design (a cylinder?) which is partly dismantled.

JENNER: [*Continues*]—that one, the one they're dismantling. It was almost new when I first left home. You natives probably share my opinion that a planet is not a fit place to live compared to a Wheel City. As you travel the worlds of the Léshy trade circuit you will have ample opportunity to confirm that opinion. The only other Wheel Cities on the circuit are in the Sol system, circling Earth in Luna's Trojan points.

You won't like them quite as well. Ah, it's not that Earth doesn't build good cities. It's the sunlight. Sol is a yellow dwarf star; if you look at it without a filter it'll burn your eyes out. We can look at Ross 614 even in naked space. In fact, on Miramon Lluagor itself we can't get plants to grow at all. A red dwarf star doesn't put out enough sunlight.

Pointer goes off.

CAPTAIN: Ready for takeoff. Hurry it up, Jenner. [*Softly*]

JENNER: [*Softly*] Yes ma'am. [*Resume normal loudness*] We're going to pull clear of the Wheel City cluster before we turn on the TRF. The Time Retarding Field is the widget that allows us to make this trip in an hour instead of a year. Within the

TRF we will become as stone statues while the rest of the universe goes on without us. You'll see time hugely accelerated. It makes for a more interesting trip. You'll at least see things moving, and you won't have time to get bored.

During the following speech, the Wheel City cluster slides off to the right, slowly, then accelerating. One spacecraft passes very close, and it's an Enzmann-type craft. The planet Miramon Lluagor slides away. The sun Ross 614 begins to shrink.

JENNER: [*Continues*] Incidentally,—Look off to your right, quick. That's probably the oldest spacecraft in human space, even older than *Queen Moriah* herself. In case of a *real* disaster, it could carry twenty thousand people to some kind of safety. It hasn't gone anywhere in a couple of hundred years, but we keep it in shape anyway.

The Enzmann ship passes offstage.

JENNER: [*Continues*] I was going to say that if the man next to you is wearing a spacesuit, it isn't a man. Or a woman. That is the only alien passenger on board this trip, one Hachuktif by name, an ambassador from an F7 star some [Never decided] light-years away. Don't irritate him. He has ambassadorial status.

Now the wheel cities are dots, and the planet itself is shrinking.

JENNER: As Miramon Lluagor dwindles astern, some of you may be beginning to have doubts. Your reasons for becoming starfarers must be numerous, and they are all good. Some of you believe that your skills, ordinary enough in your home systems, will be enormously valuable on some other world. You are correct. A few of you may have been considered homely since the day of your birth. If you feel that the citizens of another solar system will have different standards of beauty, that they may even consider you exotically beautiful or handsome, you're right again. If you love variety, if you're eager to view the many ways humanity has of being human, if you long for strange sunsets and stranger landscapes, welcome to the club. I made that decision a couple of hundred years ago in your time, eight years ago by the compressed time I live by, and I've never regretted it.

It's quite true that you can't go home again. The universe goes on without us. If you go—

Diagram of the Léshy circuit, framed, stars labeled.

JENNER: [*Continues*]—entirely around the six systems of the Léshy circuit, you will cover [Never decided] light-years and lose a dozen years more through speeding up and slowing down. You won't feel those years because of the TRF, but your world will be weirdly changed by the time you return, and if you're thinking of looking up your old girl friend, forget it—

CAPTAIN: [*Interrupts*] Ready with the TRF.

JENNER: Okay. Please watch astern.

Ross 614 abruptly shrinks like a punctured balloon.

JENNER: Fun, huh? The only thing to watch from now on is the stars. As we continue to edge closer and closer to the speed of light, the stars ahead will be blue-shifted, and stars behind us will be red-shifted until you can't see them, and to the side you'll see them creeping forward until they form the famous "starbow."

If you don't get off at Toupan, in Procyon system—

Light pointer indicates that leg of Léshy circuit.

JENNER: [*Continues*]—then our next stop is Earth, in Sol system. At this point you can stop, or go on, or—

Add two other trade circuits to the diagram.

JENNER: [*Continues*]—you can transfer to one of the other trade circuits. In all, humanity has colonized sixteen worlds, and the trade circuits all link at Sol system—by one of those interesting coincidences. If your heart surges with pride because you belong to a great interstellar empire, you might remember that all of human-occupied space is embedded in the Chirpsithra Empire.

Add every red dwarf star in the area to that diagram!

JENNER: [*Continues*] The Chirpsithra—I won't even try to pronounce their own name for themselves. I tried it once and I literally dislocated my jaw. Okay?—the Chirpsithra have a secret worth stealing. They evolved on a planet circling a red dwarf star. They have therefore spent their time colonizing the planets of red dwarf stars. Half the stars in the universe are red dwarves. One day all the stars in the universe will be red dwarves, excluding the neutron stars and black holes, and the Chirpsithra will hardly notice we are gone.

They don't like us going through their section of space, and in fact we had a heck of a time persuading them to let us stay in Ross 614 system. They occupy the next planet outward from Miramon Lluagor. The reason you weren't invited to visit them is, they don't like tourists either.

Diagram off. The stars have been red-shifting and blue-shifting in the appropriate directions, and creeping gradually forward. Slowly! And they will continue to do so.

JENNER: [*Continues*] It strikes me that you may be interested in your vehicle. In case you slept through the approach,

Queen Moriah, *framed.*

JENNER: [*Continues*] *Queen Moriah* looks like this. You are here—

Light pointer points amidships.

JENNER: [*Continues*]—surrounded by masses of metal and hydrogen fuel for maneuvering. If the ramscoop generators should break down, which perish forbid, that shielding should give us some time to try to fix them before the gamma rays cremate us. The electromagnetic generators—

Light pointer indicates forward half of ship, then goes off.

JENNER: [*Continues*]—form half the mass of the ship. What they do for us is, they scoop in the hydrogen molecules throughout interstellar space for a thousand miles around us—

Queen Moriah *picture off, replaced by a diagram of how a Bussard ramjet spacecraft works.*

JENNER: [*Continues*]—guide it into a ring-shaped constriction behind us, where the hydrogen undergoes fusion and blasts back at the stars. That's our thrust. Our fuel is free once we get up to speed, which is about twelve hundred kilometers per second. Beyond that we can accelerate forever—theoretically. In practice there'll be hell to pay if we don't go on to Procyon system as planned.

Diagram off. Light pointer runs from dead ahead to dead behind during Jenner's next speech.

JENNER: [*Continues*] You'll notice that the starbow is just beginning to take shape, with the stars getting bluer *here*, creeping forward *here*, reddening *here*. It won't ever get really vivid this trip, because we're never going to be going fast enough. We're approaching the midpoint turnover already; it's about five minutes away within the Time Retarding Field.

Light pointer off. Sound effect: Click!

JENNER: That ought to hold 'em. [*Voices have softened.*]

CAPTAIN: You and your propaganda routines. Jenner, do you really think you can talk the whole universe into building Wheel Cities?

JENNER: [*Thinks it over, then, pugnaciously*] Yeah!

CAPTAIN: Forget it. You *know* why you guys built Wheel Cities in that system. It's because your sun is a lousy little red dwarf. Your planet is uninhabitable. You can't grow anything on Miramon Lluagor because you can't get enough ultraviolet through the atmosphere. If you could live on that planet you'd be doing it.

JENNER: [*Has been trying to interrupt*] Not me. I like to know when it's going to rain. I don't like snow and I don't like tornados and I don't like earthquakes and I don't like insects that bite.

CAPTAIN: [*Interrupts, derisively*] Soft.

JENNER: Captain, do you enjoy getting caught in a snowstorm? We *control* our environments!

CAPTAIN: Your Wheel Cities make you soft. Pampered.

JENNER: I could say the same thing about your electric toothbrush. Whoops! Captain, the intercom's on.

CAPTAIN: Well, turn it off!

JENNER: It doesn't go off. Seems to be broken. Ah . . . ladies and gentlemen, it seems you're going to have to listen to us all the way to Procyon system. We'll try to be as entertaining as possible. We'll get the intercom fixed at Toupan.

[*Voice lowered*] Captain, do you ever get the feeling this ship is falling apart around us?

CAPTAIN: Better the intercom than the ramscoop generators.

JENNER: [*Thoroughly amused*] I'll buy that.

Pause. Sound effect: Clunk! Metal-on-metal.

CAPTAIN: What—

Sound effect: Zzap!

Sound effect: Captain's body hits the deck.

JENNER: Captain? [*Pause*] [*Jenner is frightened, trying to control it*] Hachuktif. You know quite well that you're not allowed in the control section.

ALIEN: I know that I am also not allowed to carry firearms.

JENNER: What is that thing? A gun? Is she dead?

ALIEN: She is not dead yet. She should have medical treatment within six hours. Medical facilities exist on my world.

JENNER: What?

ALIEN: Is my translator working? We are going to my world, Paftuchuk, circling the star [Never decided]. You will turn the ship in the direction of [Never decided].

JENNER: You can't hijack *Queen Moriah!*

ALIEN: I can shoot you and try to fly *Queen Moriah* myself.

JENNER: Wait a minute. You don't know what you're doing. You'd be steering us into Chirpsithra space! They'll—

ALIEN: Turn the ship now.

The sky begins to wheel around. Stops.

ALIEN: You will now reassure the passengers.

JENNER: Great! What do I tell them?

ALIEN: I will tell them myself. Open the intercom.

JENNER: It's already open.

ALIEN: This is your new captain speaking. When you boarded *Queen Moriah* you hoped for new environments, new and unique experiences. Your hopes are fulfilled. You felt that your skills and your professions would be very valuable in a new environment. They will be. My people of Paftuchuk have achieved spaceflight and some control of the other worlds of our system, but interstellar flight was beyond us until the coming of a human exploration ship. We need your skills.

Moriah *continues to accelerate. Starbow grows tighter and more vivid.*

JENNER: Are you making us slaves?

ALIEN: You will live in luxury. Would I have taken this risk if I did not think you immensely valuable?

JENNER: I know all about your world. If you think we can breathe that gunk you call air—

ALIEN: You will live under domes, of course.

JENNER: It's all academic anyway. We're about to enter Chirpsithra space. They'll burn us out of the sky.

ALIEN: Do you intend to cheat me? You told the passengers that all of human space is Chirpsithra space. How can they be angry if your ships cross more of Chirpsithra space?

JENNER: There are *treaties*, you glorified nightmare! We—

ALIEN: Reassure the passengers, Jenner

JENNER: [*Pause, then sarcasm*] Sure. [*Voice slightly louder*] You are passengers aboard the first interstellar spacecraft ever to be hijacked. I did promise you you wouldn't be bored, and that's the good news. Our new captain has certainly lost his ambassadorial status. His species looks like this—

Sketch of a Paftuchukian (framed).

JENNER: [*Continues*]—and Hachuktif looks a lot like that, except for the large gun. His world is scarcely more reassuring. It's an uninhabitable world under a hot star. The sun will look like a pinpoint bright enough to burn holes in your retinae, unless these primitives thought of putting a filter on the dome. The planet's atmosphere is about three percent carbon dioxide, and the smog is thick enough to smoke in a pipe. Gravity is one point three, which means we're all about to gain some unneeded weight. Because if *we* don't have antigravity, the Paftuchukians *certainly* don't.

Sketch off. The starbow has grown quite vivid and tight. Ahead, the stars blaze violet. They fade back through the spectrum to red. In a wide circle dead aft, they fade out completely. On that black circle three white points show clearly. They seem to be doing a kind of dance: Two dots merge for a few seconds, then separate, and a different pair emerge.

ALIEN: We hoped that you would have antigravity.

JENNER: Sure, and faster-than-light travel, and immortality and time travel? Sorry to disappoint you. [*To passengers*] Incidentally, you will notice that we're edging very near the speed of light. The starbow effect has become pronounced. I've never seen it like this. Behind us all the stars have been red-shifted to black, except for those three Chirpsithra warships coming up our tail.

ALIEN: I apologize. You did not lie. Can they catch us?

JENNER: They sure as—*Yahh!*

A Chirpsithra laser beam hits Moriah. *Audience is bathed in green light that lasts about a second before going out.*

JENNER: [*Excited, breathless*] I can't keep dodging forever. Did they do any damage? No, I guess not. Their laser cannons aren't as powerful as they should be. They're used to less light than we are.

[*Savagely*] All right, *Captain*, now what?

ALIEN: Can they catch us?

JENNER: Of course. They're burning each other's exhausts.

ALIEN: I don't understand.

Diagram of Bussard ramjet effect, used earlier. As Jenner speaks, substitute diagram of double Bussard ramjet effect.

JENNER: Look. We scoop in interstellar hydrogen from a thousand miles around and fuse it partially to helium. So do the Chirpsithra ships. But they put a second ship behind the first. The second ship narrows the focus of its ramscoop field, so that it scoops in the already heated exhaust for a couple of *hundred* miles around. That way they can narrow the construction too, for better fusion. The exhaust is already as hot as the center of a star. It fuses beautifully. It gives them terrific acceleration.

ALIEN: But the second ship would ram the first ship, or fly past it.

JENNER: Sure. They're playing leapfrog across space, taking turns burning each other's exhaust. You bet your life they can catch us.

ALIEN: What can you do?

The lights of the Chirpsithra warships are gradually getting brighter.

JENNER: [*Slowly*] I can watch your face until you give me that gun.

ALIEN: I will kill you.

JENNER: Then what? Have *you* thought of a way out of this?

ALIEN: Your passengers will die for your stupidity.

JENNER: Better dead than slave. I'm sure the passengers would agree.

Long pause. Then the planetarium flares with green light.

ALIEN: Turn the ship! Turn the ship! Here, I give you the gun, now turn the ship!

Green light goes out.

JENNER: How did you get into the control room, anyway?

ALIEN: I burned a hole through the ceiling of the passenger compartment. Man, the warships are closer. What can we do?

JENNER: Sit down. Fold your hands behind your neck. All of them. Keep them there. [*Pause*] I'm heading for a neutron star.

ALIEN: What is a neutron star?

JENNER: [*Laughs*] You really *are* primitives, aren't you?

All right. Some stars collapse under their own weight after they've burned up all their fuel. You find an object as massive as, say, Sol, but it's a flattened sphere no more than ten kilometers thick. Usually it's got a tremendous spin, one to ten times a second. If the original star carried a magnetic field, then so does the neutron star, and with that terrific spin it gives off pulses of X-rays. We call it a pulsar.

The one we're headed for, BVS-2,—

Light-pointer indicates, but nothing shows there.

JENNER: [*Continues*]—is a little different. Somehow it's lost most of its spin. It doesn't pulse, and of course there's no way to *see* the thing. It's as small as the average asteroid. We only found it very recently. We had no idea there was a neutron star that close to Léshy space.

Green flash, very brief.

JENNER: [*Continues as if nothing had happened*] But BVS-2 doesn't have those terrific energies churning around it.

We can get close enough without the ramscoop generators exploding.

ALIEN: But what good can it do us?

JENNER: [*Annoyed*] It's a point-mass! It'll whip us right around. It's the only way in Creation to make a sharp right-angled turn in deep space. If the warships don't follow our course exactly, they'll be scattered in all directions.

ALIEN: If you come too close, the tidal effect would—

JENNER: —Would rip us apart, right. Grab hold of something.

There's no warning of the neutron star's approach. It flashes suddenly out of the region of the blue-shifted stars: an orange disc exploding into view and as suddenly gone.

The sky has turned ninety degrees.

One of the following dots is gone. The other two are still in that black area of drastically red-shifted stars.

JENNER: Now put your hands behind your head. *Now!* Good.

ALIEN: The warships are still there.

JENNER: [*Laughs nervously*] They are, aren't they? [*Pause*] I wish I could fly a ship that well.

Brief flash of green light.

JENNER: [*Venomously*] Nuts!

ALIEN: Can you turn and run for the human worlds?

JENNER: We're headed almost for Léshy space now, but there are some problems. For one thing, we're moving too fast. We'll go right through the Léshy circuit and out. Anyway, the other problem is, those warships are going to catch us before we get there. The only reason we can keep dodging the laser beams is the lightspeed barrier. They don't see us make our turn until a couple of months after we do it, real time.

ALIEN: What will you do?

JENNER: Why don't you just sweat it out with me? [*Pause*] I keep forgetting we've got passengers. [*Voice louder*] All right, gang, I'd be lying if I said we aren't in trouble. The Chirpsithra warships can fry us if they get close enough, and I'm fresh out of neutron stars.

What I'm going to try next is a little risky. Bear with me while I do a little computer work.

ALIEN: My arms are getting tired.

JENNER: [*Abstractedly*] Imagine my delight—[*Pause*] Okay, we can do it. [*To audience*] We can do it. There's a system almost ahead of us called [Never decided]. It's a red giant and a white dwarf, orbiting very close.

Diagram of the "Flinger" system

JENNER: [*Continues*] The dwarf is orbiting at terrific speed, as you might expect. So is *Queen Moriah*. If I can bring the ship in on the right path—*this* path—

Show the path. It's between the two stars, head-on to the white dwarf and nearer to that star; then around the white dwarf and straight out.

JENNER: [*Continues*]—then we'll shed half our velocity. The Chirpsithra warships can try to follow us, but I bet they don't. It's too close to suicide. We—

ALIEN: [*Interrupts*] But if it's that close to suicide—

JENNER: *Oh, shut up*. You got us into this. The warships will just keep going, still trying to decelerate. We'll head back to Toupan in Procyon system, just like your tickets say.

"Flinger" system diagram off.

The sky has been turning, reflecting Jenner's course change. The "Flinger" system appears ahead, a white dot blinking flashes of brighter white, fast. Coming fast. Jenner uses a light-pointer.

JENNER: There it is. If we do this right we'll transfer half our velocity to the blue dwarf. I'm turning off the Time Retarding Field.

Jenner's timing is good. The "Flinger" system seems to fly at our faces, then stop dead . . . but it's still coming, more slowly. The stars grow large and separate.

JENNER: Turning the Bussard ramjet . . . off. We're going to get some gamma rays, I'm afraid.

ALIEN: We'll lose control! We're falling free!

JENNER: I hate to disillusion you, but our ramscoop fields just can't handle a mass the size of a white dwarf star. If we plotted the course right, it won't matter.

Moriah *goes through "Flinger" system. System recedes, somewhat red-shifted, looking somewhat like a target: white dwarf glowing against red giant. System recedes slowly, because TRF is still off.*

JENNER: [*Vastly relieved*] O-kay. We're through. Aimed almost at Procyon. And the Chirpsithra warships are . . . still there. [*Bitterly*]

So they are: two white dots to one side of "Flinger."

ALIEN: Turn on the Time Retarding Field.

JENNER: Oh. Yeah.

TRF goes on. The "Flinger" system dwindles like a pricked balloon. The warships streak off to the side, growing brighter. They pass Moriah, *red-shifting as they do, and dwindle ahead.*

JENNER: And that takes care of that. The only thing we have to worry about is the lethal dose of gamma rays we picked up when the ramscoop was off. For that, we'll need medical attention . . . and here . . . it comes.

A violet star in the violet starfield ahead, grows rapidly. It also dims. In fact, the entire starfield loses its "starbow" distortion. The starfield to the side shifts back; the red stars aft become brighter and whiter; the blue stars ahead dim and lose the blue tinge. Procyon grows into a yellow sun. A crescent planet appears and grows large.

JENNER: TRF off.

The planet stops growing.

JENNER: [*Continues*] We have reached Toupan, just as your ticket says. However, that little side jaunt cost us about five hundred years. There's no telling what we'll find when the shuttle ships arrive—

Two shuttle ships are approaching.

JENNER: [*Continues*]—assuming they still use spaceships. Yeah, I see they do. That's a relief! Well, gang, we'll be spending a few weeks in the hospital before we get a chance to look around.

NOTES FOR THE LÉSHY CIRCUIT

1. Certain systems need to be located and distances established.
2. The Léshy circuit reads: Earth (Sol), Koschei (Tau Ceti), Horvendile (Epsilon Eridani), Sereda (Omicron 2 Eridani), Miramon Lluagor (Ross 614), Toupan (Procyon), and back to Earth. Ships travel the Léshy circuit in both directions.
3. We need only one sketch of a Paftuchukian alien. (For one funny line I gave him more than two arms, but this is not crucial.) Many STF artists draw good aliens. The best is Bonnie Dalzell.
4. Pronunciation. Hachuktif is pronounced something like a sneeze, accent on the second syllable. Paftuchuk (alien's home world) accents on the first syllable.
5. The voice of the alien must be clearly alien. There are many ways to do this. After all, what we're hearing is a mechanical translator! We get the effect we want if the recording is speeded up, Disney-chipmunk-style; or if every word is set on the key of C; or if every word is individually pronounced (as if each word has been picked from storage by a computer, but each was spoken without reference to any other word.)
6. The Captain is middle-aged, female, and tough. She's known Jenner a long time. When she puts him down for insubordination, she does it automatically, without rancor.
7. Jenner can be sarcastic, vicious, amused, frightened, etc.

When lecturing the passengers he is often sardonic. He's younger than the Captain: thirty or so.

8. Jenner frequently throws something on the screen for the passengers' benefit. It's in a frame, and he puts it where it won't hide anything really interesting. (Our own technique precisely.) If he wants to show something *preprogrammed*, like the Léshy circuit diagram, it should look more professional than spontaneous drawings like the double-Bussard-ramjet diagram.
9. Jenner's voice should sound different when he is not talking directly into the intercom (i.e., to the passengers). I've established a convention: his voice is less loud. If you have a better idea, please feel free.
10. The original name for Chirpsithra in this script was Smith-people.

TABLETOP FUSION

hen cold fusion broke into the news, *Reason Magazine* asked me for an article on how it would affect the future.

The news had gone cold by the time I turned it in. They bought it anyway, but chose not to publish it.

The subject is warming up again.

The viewpoint of the physicists here is easy to understand. They spend money like a drunken government, trying to get enough heat and pressure to make solar-style fusion work. The money is committed years in advance. They did not warm to the notion of being beaten by chemists. Now they've admitted that something is going on: They get radiation, tritium, and other indications that it ain't just chemistry. Nuclear fusion is happening at some level.

But even without that, it's a fit subject for science fiction.

When the news hit, I bought stock in platinum mines. I had to explain to my broker that I had no interest in platinum, just the mines. They're the only source of palladium. I held for a bit, then sold it. It isn't that I lost faith. But it seems that the lattice structure of the palladium electrodes somehow absorbs the shock of two deuterium nuclei becoming one helium nucleus, so that the nucleus doesn't have to spit out most the energy as a neutron. Palladium can't be the only substance with the right lattice structure.

Now my stockbroker wants to hire me. The man she actually wants is Jerry Pournelle: these were his suggestions.

I'm a science fiction writer. It always feels as if I actually know all that stuff. In May 1989 I was prepared to tell you:

The wonderful thing is that you'll know, *and* soon. *The experimental setup at the University of Utah is cheap. Pons and Fleischmann used their own money. For a hundred thousand dollars you can try it yourself! A lot of universities and laboratories will. Before I have quite finished typing, you should know whether this is another Dean Drive or a discovery to rank with the electric motor.*

Hah! A panel discussion at Baycon in San Jose in May changed my perspective.

What's the melt? Lithium deuteroxide, but was it doped with something else? Is it the deuterium that undergoes fusion, or the lithium? Or both?

Platinum and palladium electrodes seem to be the key. But "making the electrodes is a black art." You do everything right, meticulously, and you still don't know what you'll get. Panelists spoke of electrodes used for isotope separation: melted in vacuum, and recast, fifteen times! After the tenth remelting, a spectrum change indicates that the melt is still losing trapped gas!

That black art is called alchemy, and it's old. Or else it's the infant science of chaos, like weather prediction, the stock market, disease control, and a score of other undisciplined disciplines. Results are very sensitive to initial conditions. Wobble the sixth or tenth decimal place, and everything changes. A bright calm day becomes a hurricane. A vaccine that had

AIDS stopped cold hits a sudden spike in the death rate.

Pons and Fleischmann are saying very little. Their reputations are solid; their papers are not; their methods are secret pending patent applications. The brightest friends I've got are all using the word "intuition."

So here's the future. I'm making optimistic assumptions because that's what *Reason* asked for, and because it makes the most interesting story.

If tabletop fusion is real, then we know something about it.

1. A tabletop fusion plant—call it a fusor—would be a billion times cleaner (per output in kilowatts) than a hot plasma fusion plant. That makes it cleaner than every form of power now in use except hydroelectric (which is clean if you're not downstream when the dam goes) and solar.

2. Interestingly, the tabletop fusor has no more weapons potential than a teddy bear. There's not enough power output for a decent weapons laser, and if anything goes wrong, it just stops.

You can't build it bigger because there's an upper temperature limit. The fusion takes place in the crystal lattice of the palladium, where an electric charge can concentrate deuterium nuclei to an effective 10^{24} atmospheres of pressure. That's close enough to allow fusion. Swell; but if the electrodes melt (and the theory doesn't), the crystal lattice in the palladium is lost and everything stops.

So don't expect big power plants: there's no economy of scale. There's no way to make it explode either.

3. Are we talking about running a car around the world

on a quart of lithium deuteride? Today's gas-driven car always bursts into a fireball, whatever you do to it, at least in the movies. Deuterium burns like hydrogen, sure, but a quart of the stuff isn't terribly dangerous.

I can't see fusor automobiles. The fusor won't get that small, not soon.

But we might see eighteen-wheel trucks running on fusors. Small businesses and apartment buildings and individual houses could have fusors in their basements, if the price dropped enough. The big power companies would lose customers.

Eighteen-wheelers use a lot of oil. The United States produces fuel enough to run our cars ourselves, or near enough. I'm surprised that Pons and Fleischmann haven't published everything they've got, damn quick, before Iran sets a price on their heads. They can do more harm to the oil-producing nations than any novel.

Run the eighteen-wheelers on deuterium and we'll find city air growing cleaner.

With small power plants in our basements, we would attain an independence we've long thought to be lost....

Wait a minute. We've seen how difficult it is to get one of these things to work at all. Wouldn't that push the commercial product a long way into the future? and make it hellishly expensive to manufacture? and a pain in the ass to own?

Yes. Sorry. For the foreseeable future, the fusor will be a rich man's toy. And he's a survivalist. And he still hasn't stopped paying his electric bill.

Then again: *Everything* starts as a rich man's toy. *Be the first on your block....* The wealthy test new products for us. The best designs ultimately surface, dependability goes up and the price drops. Maybe by 2050 AD.

4. Don't expect high efficiency here. This is a heat engine, but we've got to keep the electrodes below the melting point. Thermodynamics tells us that the *maximum* efficiency of a heat motor depends on the ratio between operating and ambient temperature, counting from absolute zero.

That's not good, but it's not awful.

Contrast the OTEC power plant (Ocean Thermal Energy Conversion). It gets its power from the difference in temperature between the surface and bottom of an ocean. It's expected to run on a temperature difference of ten Centigrade degrees. A seabottom is always at 4° C = 277° A; so the ratio would be 10/277 = theoretical maximum of 3.6% efficiency. Lousy. But there's a lot of ocean; and seawater is *very* conductive; and because you're stirring up nutrients in the seabottom mud, the only pollution is an excess of fish. Low efficiency, clean running, infinite fuel supply . . . and OTEC remains useful, if you have a warm water ocean.

Fusors are fueled by the deuterium in water. Low efficiency, clean running, infinite fuel. We could use up all of Earth's deuterium over the next 100,000 years and not deplete the seas by much, because most seawater isn't deuterium oxide. And when we run out, the moons of the outer planets are water cores inside ice shells!

5. Still, fusors will operate best where it's *coldest*, where the heat-sink is most useful.

Hey, that's interesting! Solar power needs sunlight. An OTEC operates best in tropic summer seas. Even *orbiting* solar plants would deliver power most easily to the equator. But a fusor operates best during a six-month winter night at the Antarctic Pole!

If you put a fusor in every basement in Alaska, Siberia, Greenland, and Antarctica, and institute a regular deuterium delivery, what do you get?

Civilization. Where nothing lives, that's where you want to put your industry. What makes civilization work is a good heat-sink.

Every nation that borders the Arctic Circle is already exploiting that environment to some extent, except Canada and the United States. But fusors could make the North Pole worth having, and the South Pole worth even more (because there's land under it.) The Soviets could laugh at our warm-water ports.

6. I was in a physics class at Cal Tech the day I realized that the proper place for a power plant is Pluto. My teacher was not impressed. Bright guy, but all these decades later, he still hates science fiction.

So let's talk about space.

Launch to orbit has always been the bottleneck, and the fusor won't help us here. The power output will be too low. But "Once you're in orbit you're halfway to anywhere," said Robert Heinlein. The fusor brings everything closer.

A fusor is the obvious power plant for a lunar base, or for anyplace in the solar system that experiences long nights.

Light-sails are still the way to explore the inner solar system. But inward from Earth there's not much besides the sun. Outward from Earth, the sunlight gets thin. You want your own power supply even if you keep the sail. The black sky makes a terrific heat sink, too.

A fusor ought to work fine with an ion drive.

Your fuel supply weighs almost nothing and lasts almost forever. (You do still have to worry about reaction mass. Shall we stop at various outer moons?) The colder it gets, the better your fusor motor likes it. This is what we really need to explore Jupiter and its moon system . . . and the rest of the solar planets, and the comets of the Oort Cloud . . . and ultimately the nearer stars. The domain of the fusor-powered ion drive reaches from lunar orbit, to infinity.

Jeremy Rifkin's response was quick. Cold fusion is evil, not because of an intrinsic danger, but because any form of power encourages the destruction of the environment.

Then it all began to look like vaporware.

The fusor assuredly isn't a hoax. At worst it's a blind alley, and not even an expensive one. At best—

Have you ever wished that you'd gotten in on a fad while it still worked? We could have been on Mars with a refitted submarine, before the Dean Drive evaporated. We could have got thin on the Beef & Bourbon Diet; become indecently healthy on brown rice. We could reshape civilization with fusor power.

Anything that makes Jeremy Rifkin unhappy can't be all bad.

THE SOUTH LOS ANGELES BROADCASTING SYSTEM

There had been a bench here. It was a bus stop, labeled as one anyway; Monney remembered the bench, but it was gone. Maybe some rioters had picked it up and run it across the street to the Vietnamese grocery and thrown it in to burn.

So they sat on the curb, and Monney sat with them because he was tired. It wasn't that Charles and Harold and Nolan had anything to say. They were only repeating old words.

"Who's gonna pay for it all?"

"We are. It's our homes."

"Well, Harold, you were the one who threw—"

"I didn't burn down a thousand buildings and carry off a, what, a million—"

"Carried off what you could."

Four of the buildings were black rubble. Across the street men in suits moved purposefully around a great black rectangle; they measured, they talked, they made faces of disgust at each other. One stepped carefully through what had been a double door into what had been a market. His footsteps crunched. The others were calling him back. Dangerous.

You could see the same on other blocks. Insurance men and owners and city officials in little clusters, pretending to be thinking about rebuilding.

"Who's gonna pay for it all?" Nolan asked again.

"*This* time," Monney added. Monney was the oldest of them. He remembered Watts burning twenty-seven years ago. Money had flowed into Watts to rebuild, to turn a slum into a civilization, to see to it that this never happened again, *that* time.

Harold burst out, "How could they do that? How could they say those cops weren't guilty?"

"It was taped. It was taped."

"That jury saw the same thing we saw, didn't they?"

Long pause. "No."

"Charles?"

Charles was slow to answer. "Well, think about it. They saw the whole tape. You know anyone who saw the whole tape? On the TV they only showed that one little part."

"Beating him and beating him—"

"Wait up, Harold. Charles, you don't really know anything."

"You think they showed the whole tape?"

"What if that's all the tape there was? Eighteen seconds. It isn't as if the guy took that had time to set up the camera first."

They others nodded thoughtfully.

Monney hadn't been planning to speak, but that did it. He said, "I saw it. One of the networks showed the whole thing."

"What? I never saw that!"

"After the riot started. Don't know what you were doing, Harold. *I* went home and locked my door. One of the . . . it was CNN. They showed the whole thing."

Charles was vindicated. "Yeah! How could they let all of them cops go like that if they only knew what we know?"

"That's what's burning my ass—"

"Hold up, Harold. Monney, *what?*"

"Well, some of it wasn't like the part all the TV News was showing. King, he *runs* at the cops. They beat him down and he's up again, like nobody can stop him. Not like that poor bastard truck driver. You seen Rodney King? He's big."

"So they say they thought he was on drugs," Charles said. "Well, maybe not. But somehow they made the jury think the cops were afraid of Rodney King, right? And it was all on tape, so . . . see? Either the tape backs them up or it doesn't."

Monney said, "Sergeant, we have captured Conan the Cimmerian. You will see to his questioning under torture." They looked at him dubiously. "Like, you know you're really in trouble when. He kept getting up and coming at 'em. And then of course he didn't, but they kept beating him. But the TV never showed why."

They mulled it. Nolan said, "You're saying Channel Four caused the goddam riot?"

"Well, I didn't . . . um."

Harold loved it. "Well, that what you're *sayin'*, isn't it? They showed some of the tape and they didn't show some of the tape, and now there's—there's fifty dead and two thousand injured and a billion dollars in damage. If it's like you said, then that's—"

"Yeah."

"So find a lawyer and sue!"

Charles shrugged angrily. Monney said, "Class action?"

"You couldn't find no lawyer to take that," Harold said. Which made Monney laugh. Charles nodded glumly.

"No no no," Monney said. "You stand at any crosswalk in any city and throw a brick, you hit six lawyers before you ever break a window. Look, all the law offices here are burned down, what are the lawyers gonna do? Damn right you can find a lawyer. Class action, yeah. You was asking, who's gonna pay to rebuild?"

Nolan said, "Channel Nine sent someone down here, he asked, why aren't you rioting? And they did. With a helicopter right over them to take the pictures."

"Could have been famous, Harold," Monney said.

Charles was looking doubtful. Starting to take this seriously. "It's . . . no, look. A billion dollars in damage, right? This isn't one of those things where you never worked in your life but you want six million dollars 'cause you fucked up your knee slipping on somebody's lawn—"

"But you settle for six hundred—"

"There really *was* a billion dollars burned out here. You can see it just walking around, *smell* it, and it's more if you count up hospital bills too, funeral expenses. You couldn't ask for less, man, they guilty or they ain't. A billion dollars."

Monney was chuckling quietly. He said, "The networks don't have that."

"Yeah, yeah, that's what I mean. You wouldn't wind up rebuilding shit!" Charles, shouting, stood and waved with both arms at the rubble around him. Within the great black rectangle, the owner and insurer and city official stopped crunching around, looked at him, then looked away. "Wouldn't build anything. You wouldn't get money. You'd wind up owning one of the networks."

Monney stared. "The ghetto owning the news?"

Harold said, "Ghetto. I been in other cities. I seen—Well, maybe it's a ghetto now."

You couldn't breathe without knowing where you were. Charred wet furniture stuffing and wood and glue and plastic. A war zone smelled like this.

"Could turn interesting, couldn't it?" Charles stood up. "A law office is what we want."

Nolan's wide white grin. "A building still standing is what we want."

"No," said Monney. They had him now, they'd sucked him in. He stood, looked around him. "Look for a new car and a suit. That won't be a pimp, not here, not yet. If it isn't a big group like *them*, it'll be a lawyer."

"And he'll look at us coming at him—"

That made a picture, all right. Still. "We can try. Charles, what is it you think you'll lose? There's nothing left."

Charles nodded; Harold shoved his hands hard into his jacket pockets like he was trying to crush rats; Nolan started walking. There weren't any new cars in sight. They would have to look elsewhere.

Monney said, "Fuck, can't you just see it? Live from beautiful downtown Watts, it's the 'Tonight Show!'" And among the blackened shells, under the sooty sky, he tried to make himself see it.

©AUSTIN-93

IT'S ONLY A STORY

NOTE: This story was written for an anthology called *The Midnight Miracle*, in which a young boy (Jason) is magically visited on Christmas Eve by the ghost of Charles Dickens, who has selected Jason for a very special mission: to create a storybook about helping Mother Earth. Larry Niven is one of twelve authors invited to participate in the storybook. In order to help, Niven informs Jason that he needs to speak to Dickens' ghost and Jason at the same time.

He was dozing in his reading chair when the timer beeped in the pocket of his sweater. Why had he set that? Then the doorbell rang and he remembered. *Midnight.*

He went to the door. "Hi, Jason. Did you get—Oh." Funny, he'd thought Jason was alone on his doorstep, until the shadows shifted.

"I am not accustomed to being *summoned*," Charles Dickens said coldly. "Did you think to brag that you had seen a ghost, sir? Or are you a skeptic, and did you think to brag that you had not?"

"No, no, I needed *you*," Larry Niven said. "I need to talk about money."

Jason was already inside, shivering a little, looking about him at walls hung with strange paintings. The ghost's eyes flicked to Jason, and he understood. A ten-year-old might not understand money, not yet; not without help.

Charles Dickens seemed not much past thirty now, and quite solid. His clothing bulked him larger yet. He wore layer after layer of clothing of the Regency era, the age when Dickens had been young.

Easier to think of him as a visiting time traveler, Niven thought, than a ghost. He said, "Enter freely and of your own will. Would you like a cappuccino?"

Dickens' ghost found a chair big enough for him; he settled into it. He asked, "Is that something Italian?" with a trace of disapproval.

"It's steamed milk with strong coffee. Making cappuccino gives my hands something to do while I think."

"Very well. Mr. Niven, Jason and I must act to save the world from threats I only half-understand. Whatever the cost, we must act. A prudent man must still discuss the price, I suppose. Is that your intent?"

"Price is one thing. You'd want to decide how to spend the money, too. There are good bets and bad."

"Yes, you might lose the money and the Earth too." Dickens smiled. "Well, then, how would you spend the price of the Earth?"

"I would leave the Earth."

Dickens pursed his lips. "Jason has told me that this is not quite a madman's dream. But why?"

"Rocket ships are so neat."

"Seriously, sir."

"Are strip mines serious? And coal-fired power plants, that store their waste products in human lungs? We do bad things to the Earth to make a profit, when the wealth of eternity is right over our heads. The real money is in deep space, out where there aren't any victims."

"Jason tells me that your rocket ships are expensive."

"We think we can make them much cheaper. Look, suppose I tell you that without space travel, any attempt to save the Earth is simply silly?" Niven twisted a knob on the cappuccino machine, and the machine howled in torment.

Dickens laughed at the dramatic maneuver. He raised his voice over the howl of steam jetting into milk. "Perfect! Say on."

Niven offered a cup to Dickens and took one himself. White foam covered it, and speckles of chocolate. "Eight worlds," he said. "Forty or fifty moons. Tens of thousands of asteroids. Comets in the billions. None of these places have air you can breathe, but we think we know how to reshape Mars or Venus—"

"Why not wait," Dickens said, "and save our own world first?" He had no trouble holding the cup, or sipping from it.

"It's called terraforming. Shape a planet until it resembles the Earth. Reshape the atmosphere until humans can breathe it. Free the drinkable water. Make the soil grow Earthly crops. Mr. Dickens, we're going to have to terraform the Earth. We need to repair the damage we've done and the damage we'll do. We need Mars and Venus as test beds for our techniques. We'd be crazy to practice on the Earth itself."

"You tell large stories."

"I don't have to pay for special effects. Just paper. Let me tell you another, or . . . Jason, *you* tell him. Can you tell Mr. Dickens about the Dinosaur Killer?"

Niven's coffee tables were scattered with small puzzles and toys. The boy was playing with a spinning disk that reflected light in evanescent rainbows. He looked up at once. "The Earth got hit by an asteroid. Wham! Sixty-five million years ago. Killed almost everything. Before that there were hundreds of kinds of dinosaurs. Now they're all dead."

Niven said, "Millions upon millions of tons of rock and metal hit somewhere on the Earth, moving at between ten and seventy miles per second. The shock wave was almost beyond imagination. Most of the life on Earth died, and half the species—the *kinds* of life. It all had to grow back."

"Like Noah's Ark," Dickens said.

"Yeah, if Noah was drunk enough to forget to take the unicorns and fairies. But that happens constantly. Nature is criminally wasteful."

"Could you stop such a thing today?"

"No. We might find a way to survive several months of night—"

Dickens said, "But you have, er, neat ships that travel through space."

"Barely. We couldn't stop a Dinosaur Killer asteroid. We'd have trouble fixing anything at all. There are well-meaning people whose love and fear for Mother Earth far outweigh their judgment and education. They're wasting their time on hoodoos—no offense, Mr. Dickens. They're *terrified* of a periodic hole in the ozone layer above Antarctica, that forms every winter when the carbon dioxide freezes out above an active volcano. They block nuclear power plants, the safest form of power we know how to use. They yanked all the *apples* out of our *schools* because of a harmless pest killer called Alar! They're ignoring the real dangers, the real reasons for putting a colony somewhere off Earth."

"Mr. Niven, are you afraid of another falling mountain?"

"No," Niven said. "That's not a bad argument, but no. Let me tell you another story. The sun and the Earth and the other planets all formed out of a whirlpool of gas and dust, five billion years ago. The universe—stars, galaxies, everything—all formed *fifteen* billion years ago. We know it only takes five billion years to make a tool-using species—"

"How, sir?"

"We *have* one. Us, mankind. From gas cloud to mankind, five billion years."

"Ah."

"So the first tool users should have reached our level of development ten billion years ago."

Dickens smiled. "Ours, sir?"

Niven didn't smile. "Yes, yours in 1800s England, mine a breath later. Two hundred years is trivial on such a scale. From horse-drawn carriages to cars and airplanes? It's the blink of an eye.

"There must have been other species evolving, and some took other paths and still became intelligent. The, um, call them Wizards, were the first tool builders. We don't care what shape they were. They found atomic power before they ran out of chemical power, and fusion power a breath later, but they found it easiest to take the power of their sun.

"Maybe there are species that would quit at that point. Stay home, restrict their population, stop building. The ones who didn't are the ones we're calling Wizards, the ones we're interested in, because we can find them.

"They're the ones who build colonies on all their planets and habitats in between. Ultimately they need the total output of their star. They block every beam of sunlight. After the energy runs through their generators they let it leak to space, but at a much lower temperature. You can't use energy unless there's someplace to dump it."

Dickens asked, "Where are they now? Would your Wizards have visited the Earth?"

Niven said, "They would have had to wait for the Earth and sun to condense out of the dust. Ten billion . . . well, let's be fair, it's less than that. Everything that makes up a planet is stuff that blasts out of exploding stars. We have to wait for some early stars to explode before we get any planets. But give them three billion years and they'll still be seven billion years ahead of us, and yes, they could visit us.

"Or *we* could find *them*. If they were nearby, we'd find an object radiating the energy of a star, but in deep infrared, at the temperature of lukewarm water. If they're halfway across the universe from us, they're still billions of years advanced beyond us, and they're tool users. They'll have enclosed all the stars throughout whole galaxies. We'd find them that way."

"Wonderful."

"But we haven't found them," Niven said.

"You might continue looking?"

"There should be millions of Wizard civilizations. They should be conspicuous. It's the most interesting mystery we know. It's Enrico Fermi's question: *Where are they?*"

"It's your story, sir."

"Where are all the galactic empires? Is there something that eats tool users? Maybe they kill each other off in wars as soon as they've got fission or fusion bombs or something more powerful."

"I don't know of these weapons."

"They're like little suns brought to earth. All my life, we've been waiting for my country and the Soviets to cover the world in radioactive fireballs. We have weapons to smash cities, but for forty-five years we never used them, and now the Soviet Union's gone bankrupt. It looks like tool users don't have to bomb themselves into extinction."

"Good news."

"Damn right. But let's talk about money."

"Ah, now we come to it. You said that the wealth of eternity is over our heads."

"Oh, it's there. Easy to prove. Jason? How do we know about the Dinosaur Killer?"

Jason turned from a line of statuettes, alien life forms in ceramics and clay. "Iridium? There was iridium in the asteroid. Whapping the Earth vaporized it, spread it all over. There's a half-inch of clay, some places. . . ."

Niven said, "The Cretaceous-Tertiary boundary is the layer of dead clay above the dinosaur bones, below the beginning of the Age of Mammals. The Alvarezes, father and son, looked for iridium in the clay to see if volcanoes might have killed the dinosaurs. They found too much iridium. There's a lot more in asteroids and comets than in volcanos. It's heavy, it sinks to the center of planets. Iridium, that's valuable, isn't it, Jason?"

"Yeah."

"See, the metal in the average metallic asteroid matches all the refined metals used on Planet Earth for the last five years. Now, keep your eye on the pound note."

"I shall be your Ebenezer Scrooge."

"Yeah. Scrooge paid Cratchit a decent wage, didn't he? For the time, good money?"

"Of course. I never meant to suggest that Ebenezer Scrooge was dishonest."

"Good. Did Jason tell you anything about the double helix? Genetics?"

"No."

"Mr. Dickens, we've learned something about the forces that shape us in the womb. We'll learn more. Ultimately we'll be reshaping ourselves."

"What would you reshape? Were we not made perfect?"

"Well. Specifically? I have a friend, Tricia Harrison. For years she suffered from lupus. It's a terrible disease, and it's genetic. The doctors got it under control, for awhile. Then they thought it had come back. Agony in her back had her nearly paralyzed. They wasted more years thinking it was lupus and treating her for that. What was happening was bone growth in her spine."

Suffering was not a new concept to Charles Dickens. His eyes softened, but he only nodded, and Niven went on.

"What it took to get her any relief at all was three operations on parts of her spine, to scrape the bone out of the spinal channel. She has to heal some before they do the third one. What it *might* have taken is tailored viruses.

"Natural viruses are diseases like the common cold. The virus enters a cell nucleus and rewrites the instructions there, so the cell—the whole body—grows differently. In principle we can rewrite the instructions in the virus so that it will cure lupus, or stop the bone growth in a lady's spine.

"Now, that's advanced fine-tuning. A cure for the diabetes that killed my friend Dan Alderson would sell better, and on that basis we'll have it sooner—"

The ghost stared at him. "Man, do you hear the arrogance in what you say? Every man owes God a death. Do you think you've become God, to forgive that debt?"

The steam jet howled. Niven was making cappuccino again, perhaps to give him time to think. Then he said, "We've already got microbes making medicine for us. There's an alga that can cause an oil spill at sea to clump up so we can get rid of it. It shouldn't be that difficult to make a parasite to sterilize a mosquito, or a microbe that can eat diffuse gasoline fumes before the sunlight turns it to smog.

"Mr. Dickens, you might convince *me* that we shouldn't be doing this. *I* see the danger, even if I approve of the arrogance. But who will you convince next? Five billion of us, one at a time? Nobody who knows them could let Tricia Harrison suffer or Dan Alderson die. The rewards for success are very great, and we've been doing it for a hundred thousand years."

"Conquering other worlds is one thing, but—*What* did you say?"

"Reshaping life forms is an old, old art form. There are a thousand recognized breeds of dogs on Earth. They were all shaped by selective breeding. The Chinese can grow radishes in a wonderful variety of shapes. Broccoli and pink grapefruit are recent inventions, but wheat is as old as civilization, and it can't breed without human help.

"The human race has been twisting nature for as long as we've been human. It used to take centuries, and it's labor-intensive, but it doesn't cost much. A sheep-herding dog might cost—in Regency era money—two pounds a year for three hundred years, paying for itself every step of the way. We set rabbits loose in Australia and mongooses in Hawaii. Those were mistakes. They were cheap to make, but they cost us billions. The Sahara Forest seems to have been destroyed by sheep herding—"

"Desert, I think. Sahara Desert."

"Yeah, *now*. And there was a plan to stop the boll weevil in Texas. That *would* have been cheap next to what it's cost since." Niven waved it off. "That was then. This is now. Now we know how to trim the double helix."

"Your mistakes will become more serious, then."

"Oh, the range of possible mistakes is nothing short of *wonderful* to a writer of fiction, Mr. Dickens. But the rewards are nearly beyond the dreams of avarice. Worms that make gold dust from ore. Pigs or whatever with microbes in their bellies that can digest plastic or drink cans. But if a plastic-eating microbe got loose in the supermarkets . . . or a gold eater in Tiffany's—"

The ghost looked into Niven's eyes . . . looked into his mind, perhaps. "This is what frightens you."

"Yes. Keep your eye on the pound note, and let us consider the cost of a safe, conscientiously-run gene-twisting laboratory with adequate security in, say, Vermont in 1993. We'll say they're working on a rotifer that can clean the cholesterol plaque off of artery walls—" He saw Dickens's incomprehension, and explained, "They're hoping to stop heart failure. The lab costs, say, $100,000,000 to build and $30,000,000 a year to run."

"Just what do we mean by *safely*, now?"

"Airlocks. Redundant walls. A containment shell. Security, to stop some crazy from bringing in a bomb. We're five billion people now, and some of them are very weird, and transportation has become very easy. Even with expensive security, your laboratory *still* isn't safe, because someone in Vermont would demand that you move, and the Sierra Club would demand that you quit. So you might move, but *moving* gene-engineering equipment isn't safe either.

"Do you understand that nothing could make such a thing absolutely safe? Our civilization covers the world, Mr. Dickens. The coffee for our cappuccino came from Costa Rica, the tradition is Italian, and the machine was probably made in Taiwan. A mistake in a gene lab could cover the world in two days. Instant plague. Then, some crazies might think gene tampering is sacreligious. Evil."

"I might even agree, sir."

"Uh huh. Might you even use explosives on the lab without knowing what's in the test tubes, that might be sprayed into the air? Okay, you wouldn't. But can you believe in someone that stupid, with an airplane ticket to Vermont?"

"Is that what makes it so expensive?"

"Yeah. Damage done by rioters. Lawyers. Moving, if you're forced out. But—here's the point—what if we put the same laboratory on the Moon instead?"

Dickens considered. "A plague would not spread. There's . . . no air? And your, your crazies could not afford the tickets. But, sir, would your geneticists feel safe? What would keep them alive? Balloons full of air, imported. . . ."

"Imported from two hundred and forty thousand miles away. A village like a cluster of bubbles buried under lunar soil. If you knew that a village like that has been there for thirty or forty years, and houses two thousand people, would you feel safe about moving there? They'd have had time to make all the obvious mistakes and live through them. With that in place, a team of geneticists could live and work on the Moon in safety. Yes?"

Dickens nodded.

"The cost in money might have to be counted in trillions of dollars—millions of millions—even if we can replace the shuttles with something realistic. There are ways to make it pay for itself, but even so. By the way, they won't just shut down that lab in Vermont and wait thirty years."

"No. Every age wants results faster than that."

"The danger in gene-twisting doesn't come from Vermont anyway. A lab in Chile would be much cheaper, because you could *hide* it. You need not announce the venture to the World Federation of Nut Cases. A few bribes would take care of any cost-saving deficiencies in your safety precautions. So in terms of the creation of new and useful and *profitable* life forms, the Chile option might cost more like two million. And what do you make of that, Mr. Scrooge?"

"I suppose . . . I will build my laboratory in Chile and pocket the money. And I suppose that tells us what happened to the aliens, the Wizards."

Niven nodded. "That's what I see. 'Remember, mighty Earthling, there were others here before you.' The universe gives birth to tool users; we can't guess how often. They die out. The Wizards learned how to reshape their environment and themselves, and they made one mistake.

"They would have lived, they would be here now, if space travel was easy. Their problem was money. The cost of settling other planets is a million times the cost of tampering with their own genetic inheritance."

"*Mr. Dickens—*" Jason ran to the chair, but was afraid to touch him. Charles Dickens was fading, losing shape like colored smoke.

Niven knew he'd gone too far. "Easy now. It's only a story," he said gently. "Only science fiction. It's based on what we know, but what we know keeps changing, you know? Today this is the threat we see. George Orwell saw a threat and warned us, he wrote a book called *1984*, and we ducked that threat and went elsewhere. We can do it again."

"How? Be you the Ghost of Christmas Future. What other path do you show us?"

Niven shook his head. "Jason is the future. I'm the present, you're the past. Okay. The trick is that village on the Moon. Or the orbiting bubbles we know how to build, or space stations that circle Mars and Venus while we terraform *them*, or big hollow trees gene-shaped to grow from a comet head. *Anything.*"

"I don't . . . ah."

"You see it? One mistake in a lab in Chile, a plague covers the Earth in two days, but it can't cross vacuum. Colonies would be safe. At worst we'd have to terraform the Earth afterward. That's why we have to start reshaping Mars and Venus. We'll want the practice."

"Just a story." Dickens was solid again.

"Yeah. Just a story, for now," Niven said. "But if we can put humans where our mistakes can't infect them, can't *reach* them, we'll beat the game.

"Fifteen billion years the universe has been waiting for one of us to beat the Catch-22 of genetic engineering. The first of the tool users who *do not* make a mistake will breed gods."

INTERCON TRIP REPORT

AUGUST 12, 1991

Intercon is a once-per-two-years convention at the University of Oslo, Norway. At the Holland Worldcon they asked me to attend as the Guest of Honor from USA, with Mary Gentle from England, and two locals.

Sunday: I drove Marilyn to Los Angeles International. She's running next year's Old Lacers convention. This year's is in New Jersey. So it's Marilyn in New Jersey and her husband in Oslo.

Monday: I wrote down the exact location of the car in Lot C, phoned and left it on my answering service for Michelle Coleman to transmit to Marilyn in New Jersey.

SAS boosted me to Business Class. The seats are perfectly orthopedic when reclined, and a shelf pops up under your legs too. They'll bust your back when upright if you don't kill the curve with a pillow, but SAS supplies a pillow.

Tuesday afternoon: Landed at Oslo Airport. Nine-hour time difference. My back felt fine. The seats work!

Björn Vermo had volunteered to escort me around. He drove me to the Nobel Hotel, Then walked me around Oslo for a couple of hours. Walking after a long plane flight seems to be a powerful antidote: I felt wonderful. And I collapsed right quick.

Wednesday: The Nobel serves a wonderful breakfast,

brunchlike, terminating at 10 AM. No problem. My body had shifted by *twelve* hours, and stayed that way.

Björn drove us to Alfred Nobel's historic dynamite works, now a museum, at Eugene. Interesting. Then more.... I was still jet-lagged, dozing in the car.

He had me back by evening. I wandered the territory I'd seen Tuesday. Street music, lots of parks and fountains, a roofless restaurant.

Thursday: An old industrial site in a deep valley. "They've locked up the waterfall" in pipes running down the cliff to a power plant, all decades old. "Sometimes they let it out." There's a turbine on display, designed for not much water and a pressure head of half a mile, with a jet that could cut Superman in half.

The old captains of industry followed powerful obligations to their workers. Early this century, one noticed his people were going nuts without sunlight in winter. He set up an early cable car system to get his people up to the crest in winter, where the sunlight was.

We went up and wandered the crest for a while. Wonderful view.

Up the canyon to the power plant, and the site of the Nazi heavy water plant. Allies tried to bomb it, but the canyon's too deep. They couldn't get an angle. Norwegian saboteurs went in, blew it up, went out, a hairy exercise that ran smooth as silk. They later starred in a movie about it. The Nazis fixed the plant, we *did* bomb it, and the Nazis (believing that they needed heavy water to make their bomb) quit.

Upslope still, to a dam made with no concrete, just rock. It's a Norwegian technique. Dinner: an isolated restaurant, wonderful view, and unfamiliar but delicious fish. Then—

Bruce Pelz had warned me not to leave Norway without seeing a stave church. Björn took us to a working stave church at dusk (9 PM). It's truly wonderful, and indescribable.

Friday: Five in the morning, I woke with an allergy attack. It gets me in the eyes. Cause: fatigue, shortage of sleep. It eased off after four hours or so. I got some shopping in before Björn showed up at noon.

Oslo is surrounded by primeval forest. Björn was set to take me walking there. But Intercon was due to start at 6 PM, and my GOH speech would follow. "Get me to the hotel for a couple of hours on my back," I said, "or I'll collapse."

Nordic law allows anyone to pick berries in the forest; it's one reason the forest has to be protected with such ferocity. We ate blueberries and wild strawberries as we went. Björn took us to a tremendous view over Oslo.

Then he got us lost. Three kilometers down a wrong path, in the rain, and back too far, before he realized that he'd been reading his compass with his knife blade directly underneath it. I didn't make it back to the car. I boarded a bus a kilometer short of that target; sat around 10–15 minutes waiting for the bus to move; and saw Björn in his car at the next stop.

The hotel shower was all that I'd dreamed of during the walk in the rain. Heaven.

I'm afraid I short-changed the speech somewhat. My mind just turned off. But I'd gone for show-and-tell, because of the language gap. I'd tossed my stuff in my luggage: Ringworld Game and Comic illustrations; design specs for Dream Park paraphernalia; interesting badges; the TrantorCon Restaurant Guide; *Fallen Angels* and the T-shirt with the cover; other books;

things to pass around. I hope they spoke for me. (I think I'll try it again at my next convention.)

Saturday: Everyone in Oslo seems to speak English. It was like a standard little convention in some respects. In others, no. They take it for granted that the GOHs will vanish frequently to do tourist things.

I was lucid again for the morning panel. Then we (Björn and Mary Gentle and her husband and some others) went to lunch and the Viking Ship Museum. Viking ships are awesome in the complexity and skill of their creation.

Sirius Magazine had published one of my stories. They fed me Danish beer and Linaea Aquavit: chive-flavored vodka that has been shipped to the southern hemisphere and back (across the line) as a guaranteed means of aging. It's wonderful.

Nightfall, 9 PM: Heidi Lyshol (the energy source for Oslo fandom) and her husband took me and Mike Jitlov to Emmanuel Vigeland's Sculpture Garden. This is the right time, she says. See it in half-darkness, without swarming tourists. We wandered among over a hundred statues of people at every age and in almost every possible human mood, and not a scrap of clothing among them. Nice, somber mood.

Sunday: My back was still fine: good enough that I admitted I'd sign autographs. Good enough that I went back to Vigeland's sculpture garden to see it by daylight. Heidi's wrong. The statues fit just *fine* among a seething swarm of tourists. (One artist's vision shaped all of these, with apprentice help. They have a generic look, as if Vigeland forbade any detail beyond some level.)

When I reached the U, Mary and her husband were fighting. Swords. Demonstrating a technique they evolved themselves, swordsmanship turned on its side so that nobody gets hurt. Meanwhile, someone had made off with around $900 in convention receipts, a paper bag of Norwegian kroner clearly labeled as to value and left sitting at the desk. Oslo is delightfully crime-free, but Intercon may have to invent Security real soon now.

A Soviet publisher brought his wife with him to translate, and his one-and-a-half-year-old daughter. He wants rights to some of my books. The baby's just learning Russian. When her mother begins speaking gibberish, she flies into an instant screaming rage.

So Daddy would speak; then Mommy would begin to tell me in English what stories were wanted, conditions, terms; and the girl would begin a shrieking fit. She didn't like me talking either!

They tried various approaches. Mother retreated, nursed her, got her calm . . . return and spoke English, and BOOM.

The format that ultimately worked must have been fun to watch. Daddy's carrying the girl, swinging her, soothing her, way the hell at the far end of the hall. Back he comes, and he speaks several paragraphs of Russian to *me*. Then he's briskly off with Daughter, out of earshot while Mommy translates. I answer. Daddy swings back for more . . . a long elliptical orbit. . . .

He asked me to attend a Russian convention. Annual. In February. Sounds cold. 1992 looks busy for me, so I begged to be asked for 1993. . . .

(And now Gorbachev's down and back up, the Gang of Eight Stooges is imprisoned, and who knows?)

Two o'clock, Heidi takes us off to a *different* sculptor Vigeland's mausoleum, "the most secret museum in Europe." Pass through an outer and inner door: The tomb is dimly lit, with rows of chairs down the center. Vigeland shaped statues inappropriate to the public sculpture garden, and painted the walls with human figures, and skills, and his own portrait twice, living and dead. Every door handle is a snake in a unique configuration. The urn with his ashes sits over the inner door, under the only complete skeletons in the place: They're fucking in missionary position. It's awesome, it's somber, it shouldn't be missed.

As the convention wound down, so did I. After closing, a handful of us retreated to Ellen Andresen's for dinner. I was nearly comatose. Dinner was late but both good and strange, built around hot cereal with a sour cream base. And Heidi took us (me and Mike Jitlov) home.

Monday: I packed the bottle of Pan liqueur Björn gave me. But I found and bought Linaea Aquavit duty-free. Now my backpack weighs a ton.

The plane takes off at 10:30, no sweat, bound south for Copenhagen. I'll change planes and double back over the north pole.

Yeah ... but they can't get our plane to start. From 12:30 they've postponed to 7:00. But they've arranged to take us all to lunch at Tivoli Gardens. It could be worse. I didn't phone Marilyn yet; it was 3 AM in Los Angeles.

Three buses reached Tivoli. I'd forgotten where we were bound for, so I just stuck with the crowd ... and lost them, and may have gotten two other passengers lost too. Two twenty-year-old girls, one from California, one from Sweden. We did our best to hunt down the restaurant, and finally I bought them lunch at random.

We wandered around together, then they went off to shop. My energy was dwindling. Music, flowers, games, crowds . . . and my back was starting to hurt, so I sat down a lot. I got rained on. I'd checked my backpack at the airport, sweater and all. No sweat. I drank a cappuccino under a roof, and waited for sunshine.

Back aboard a bus at 5:00. The guy in front of me was a fan, had gone to college with Alex Pournelle, and was just starting Brin's *Earth*, which I had finished on the trip. He had some data for me if I ever planned to go to Russia. We talked a little. He says he's very prone to coincidence. . . .

And SAS had postponed to 7:30, to use a plane due in from Japan.

I asked for the return of the money I'd spent on three lunches, and an SAS man got it for me. I bought a haircut, and a ton of chocolate. I phoned Marilyn.

It took off on time. They boosted me forward again: reclining seats. The guy next to me was an engineer with an intense interest in the sciences and none in science fiction. A fascinating conversationalist. We all pretended to sleep, as the plane flew through an endless whiteout afternoon. . . .

And when the flight was over, my back had stopped hurting. I LOVE SAS.

Marilyn met me, jet-lagged herself on New Jersey time, and drove us home. I opened the bottle of Pan. It's a Norwegian liqueur made from forest berries, and it's wonderful.

©AUSTIN-93

ALL THE BRIDGES RUSTING

Take a point in space.

Take a specific point near the star system Alpha Centaurus, on the line linking the center of mass of that system with Sol. Follow it as it moves toward Sol system at lightspeed. We presume a particle in this point.

Men who deal in the physics of teleportation would speak of it as a "transition particle." But think of it as a kind of super-neutrino. Clearly it must have a rest mass of zero, like a neutrino. Like a neutrino, it must be fearfully difficult to find or stop. Despite several decades in which teleportation has been in common use, nobody has ever directly demonstrated the existence of a "transition particle." It must be taken on faith.

Its internal structure would be fearfully complex in terms of energy states. Its relativistic mass would be twelve thousand two hundred tons.

One more property can be postulated. Its location in space is uncertain: a probability density, thousands of miles across as it passes Proxima Centauri, and spreading. The mass of the tiny red dwarf does not bend its path significantly. As it approaches the solar system the particle may be found anywhere within a vaguely bounded wave front several hundred thousand miles across. This vagueness of position is part of what makes teleportation work. One's aim need not be so accurate.

Near Pluto the particle changes state.

Its relativistic mass converts to rest mass within the receiver cage of a drop ship. Its structure is still fearfully complex for an elementary particle: a twelve-thousand-two-hundred-ton spacecraft, loaded with instruments, its hull windowless and very smoothly contoured. Its presence here is the only evidence that a transition particle ever existed. Within the control cabin, the pilot's finger is still on the TRANSMIT button.

Karin Sagan was short and stocky. Her hands were large; her feet were small and prone to foot trouble. Her face was square and cheerful, her eyes were bright and direct, and her voice was deep for a woman's. She had been thirty-six years old when *Phoenix* left the transmitter at Pluto. She was three months older now, though nine years had passed on Earth.

She had seen a trace of the elapsed years as *Phoenix* left the Pluto drop ship. The shuttlecraft that had come to meet them was of a new design, and its attitude jets showed the color of fusion flame. She had wondered how they made fusion motors that small.

She saw more changes now, among the gathered newstapers. Some of the women wore microskirts whose hems were cut at angles. A few of the men wore asymmetrical shirts—the left sleeve long, the right sleeve missing entirely. She asked to see one man's left cuff, her attention caught by the glowing red design. Sure enough, it was a functional wristwatch; but the material was soft as cloth.

"It's a Bulova *Dali*," the man said. He was letting his amusement show. "New to you? Things change in nine years, Doctor."

"I thought they would," she said lightly. "That's part of the fun."

But she remembered the shock of relief when the heat struck. She had pushed the TRANSMIT button a light-month out from Alpha Centaurus B. An instant later sweat was running from every pore of her body.

There had been no guarantee. The probability density that physicists called a transition particle could have gone past the drop ship and out into the universe at large, beyond rescue forever. Or . . . a lot could happen in nine years. The station might have been wrecked or abandoned.

But the heat meant that they had made it. *Phoenix* had lost potential energy entering Sol's gravitational field and had gained it back in heat. The cabin felt like a furnace, but it was their body temperature that had jumped from 98.6° to 102°, all in an instant.

"How was the trip?" the young man asked.

Karin Sagan returned to the present. "Good, but it's good to be back. Are we recording?"

"No. When the press conference starts you'll know it. That's the law. Shall we get it going?"

"Fine." She smiled around the room. It was good to see strange faces again. Three months with three other people in a closed environment . . . it was enough.

The young man led her to a dais. Cameras swiveled to face her, and the conference started.

Q: How was the trip?

"Good. Successful, I should say. We learned everything we wanted to know about the Centaurus systems. In addition, we learned that our systems work. The drop-ship method is feasible. We reached the nearest stars, and we came back, with no ill effects."

Q: What about the Centaurus planets? Are they habitable?

"No." It hurt to say that. She saw the disappointment around her.

Q: Neither of them checked out?

"That's right. There are six known planets circling Alpha Centaurus B. We may have missed a couple that were too small or too far out. We had to do all our looking from a light-month away. We had good hopes for B-2 and B-3—remember, we knew they were there before we set out—but B-2 turns out to be a Venus-type with too much atmosphere, and B-3's got a reducing atmosphere, something like Earth's atmosphere three billion years ago."

Q: The colonists aren't going to like that, are they?

"I don't expect they will. We messaged the drop ship *Lazarus II* to turn off its JumpShift unit for a year. That means that the colony ships won't convert to rest mass when they reach the receiver. They'll be reflected back to the solar system. They should appear in the Pluto drop ship about a month from now."

Q: Having lost nine years.

"That's right. Just like me and the rest of the crew of *Phoenix*. The colonists left the Pluto transmitter two months after we did."

Q: What are the chances of terraforming B-3 someday?

Karin was glad to drop the subject of the colony ships. Somehow she felt that she had failed those first potential colonists of another star system. She said, "Pretty good, *someday*. I'm just talking off the top of my head, you understand. I imagine it would take thousands of years, and would involve seeding the atmosphere with tailored bacteria and waiting for them to turn methane and ammonia and hydrocarbons into air. At the moment it'll pay us better to go on looking for worlds around other stars. It's so bloody easy, with these interstellar drop ships."

There was nodding among the newstapers. They knew about drop ships and they had been briefed. In principle there was no difference between *Lazarus II* and the drop ships circling every planet and most of the interesting moons and asteroids in the solar system. A drop ship need not be moving at the same velocity as its cargo. The *Phoenix*, at rest with respect to Sol and the Centaurus suns, had emerged from *Lazarus II's* receiver cage at a third of lightspeed.

"The point is that you can use a drop ship more than once," Karin went on. "By now *Lazarus II* is one and a third light-years past Centaurus. We burned most of its fuel to get the ship up to speed, but there's still a maneuver reserve. Its next target is an orange-yellow dwarf, Epsilon Indi. *Lazarus II* will be there in about twenty-eight years. Then maybe we'll send another colony group."

Q: Doctor Sagan, you were as far from Sol as anyone in history has ever gotten. What was it like out there?

Karin giggled. "We were as far from any star as anyone's ever gotten. It was a long night. Maybe it was getting to us. We had a bad moment when we thought there was an alien ship coming up behind us." She sobered, for that moment of relief had cost six people dearly. "It turned out to be *Lazarus*. I'm afraid that's more bad news. *Lazarus* should have been decelerating. It wasn't. We're afraid something's happened to their drive."

That caused some commotion. It developed that many of the newstapers had never heard of the first *Lazarus.* Karen started to explain . . . and that turned out to be a mistake.

The first interstellar spacecraft had been launched in 2004, thirty-one years ago.

Lazarus had been ten years in the building, but far more than ten years of labor had gone into her. Her life-support systems ran in a clear line of development back to the first capsules to orbit Earth. The first fusion-electric power plants had much in common with her main drive, and her hydrogen fuel tanks were the result of several decades of trial and error. Liquid hydrogen is tricky stuff. Centuries of medicine had produced suspended-animation treatments that allowed *Lazarus* to carry six crew members with life-support supplies sufficient for two.

The ship was lovely—at least, her re-entry system was lovely, a swing-wing streamlined exploration vehicle as big as any hypersonic passenger plane. Fully assembled, she looked like a haphazard collection of junk. But she was loved.

There had been displacement booths in 2004: The network of passenger teleportation had already replaced other forms of transportation over most of the world. The cargo ships that lifted *Lazarus's* components into orbit had been fueled in flight by JumpShift units in the tanks. It was a pity that *Lazarus* could not take advantage of such a method. But conservation of momentum held. Fuel droplets entering *Lazarus's* tanks at a seventh of lightspeed would tear them apart.

So *Lazarus* had left Earth at the end of the Corliss accelerator, an improbably tall tower standing up from a flat asteroid a mile across. The fuel tanks—most of *Lazarus's* mass—had been launched first. Then the ship itself, with enough maneuvering reserve to run them down. *Lazarus* had left Earth like a string of toy balloons, and telescopes had watched as she assembled herself in deep space.

She had not been launched into the unknown. The telescopes of Ceres Base had found planets orbiting Alpha Centaurus B. Two of these might be habitable. Failing that, there might at least be seas from which hydrogen could be extracted for a return voyage.

"The first drop ship was launched six years later," Karin told them. "We should have waited. I was five when they launched *Lazarus*, but I've been told that everyone thought that teleportation couldn't possibly be used for space exploration because of velocity differences. If we'd waited we could have put a drop ship receiver cage on *Lazarus* and taken out the life-support system. As it was, we didn't launch *Lazarus II* until—" She stopped to add up dates. "Seventeen years ago. 2018."

Q: Weren't you expecting Lazarus *to pass you?*

"Not so soon. In fact, we had this timed pretty well. If everything had gone right, the crew of *Lazarus I* would have found a string of colony ships pouring out of *Lazarus II* as it fell across the system. They could have joined up to explore the system, and later joined the colony if that was feasible, or come home on the colony return ship if it wasn't"

Q: As it is, they're in deep shit.

"I'm afraid so. Can you really say that on teevee?"

There were chuckles at her naiveté.

Q: What went wrong? Any idea?

"They gave us a full report with their distress signal. There was some trouble with the plasma pinch effect, and no parts to do a full repair. They tried running it anyway—they didn't have much choice, after all. The plasma stream went wrong and blew away part of the stern. After that there wasn't anything they could do but set up their distress signal and go back into suspended animation."

Q: What are your plans for rescue?

Karin made her second error. "I don't know. We just got back two days ago, and we've spent that time traveling. It's easy enough to pump energy into an incoming transition particle to compensate for a jump in potential energy, but the only drop ship we've got that can *absorb* potential energy is at Mercury. We couldn't just flick in from Pluto; we'd have been broiled. We had to flick in to Earth orbit by way of Mercury, then go down in a shuttlecraft." She closed her eyes to think. "It'll be difficult. By now *Lazarus* must be half a light-year beyond Alpha Centaurus, and *Lazarus II* more than twice that far. We probably can't use *Lazarus II* in a rescue attempt."

Q: Couldn't you drop a receiver cage from Lazarus II, *then wait until* Lazarus *has almost caught up with it?*

She smiled indulgently. At least they were asking intelligent questions. "Won't work. *Lazarus II* must have changed course already for Epsilon Indi. Whatever happens is likely to take a long time."

Teevee was mostly news these days. The entertainment programs had been largely taken over by cassettes, which could be sold devoid of advertisements, and which could be aimed at more selective audiences.

And newspapers had died out, but headlines had not. The announcers were saying things like: *Centaurus planets devoid of life . . . colony ships to return . . . failure of* Lazarus *scout ship engines . . . rescue attempts to begin . . . details in a moment, but first this word . . .*

Jerryberry Jansen of CBA smiled into the cameras. The warmth he felt for his unseen audience was genuine: He regarded himself as a combination of entertainer and teacher, and his approximately twelve million students were the measure of his success. "The Centaurus expedition was by no means a disaster," he told them. "For one thing, the colony fleet—which cost you, the taxpayer, about six hundred and sixty million new dollars nine years ago—can be re-used as is, once the UN Space Authority finds a habitable world. Probably the colonists themselves will not want to wait that long. A new group may have to be retrained.

"As for the interstellar drop ship concept, it works. This had been the first real test, and it went without a hitch. Probably the next use of drop ships will not be a colony expedition at all, but an attempt to rescue the crew of *Lazarus.* The ship was sending its distress signal. There is good reason to think that the crew is still alive.

"Doctor Karin Sagan has pointed out that any rescue attempt will take decades. This is reasonable, in that the distances to be covered are to be measured in light-years. But today's ships are considerably better than *Lazarus* could ever have been."

"You idiot," said Robin Whyte, Ph.D. He twisted a knob with angry force, and the teevee screen went blank. A few minutes later he made two phone calls.

Karin was sightseeing on Earth.

The UN Space Authority had had a new credit card waiting for her, a courtesy she appreciated. Otherwise she would have had to carry a sackful of chocolate dollars for the slots. Her hands quickly fell into the old routine: insert the card, dial, pull it out , and the displacement booth would send her somewhere else.

It was characteristic of Karin that she had not been calling old friends. The impulse was there, and the worn black phone book with its string of nine-year-old names and numbers. But the people she had known must have changed. She was reluctant to face them.

There had been a vindictive impulse to drop in on her ex-husband. *Here I am at thirty-six, and you—* Stupid. Ron knew where she had been for nine years, so why bug the man?

She had cocktails at Mr. A's in San Diego, lunch at Scandia in Los Angles, and dessert and coffee at Ondine in Sausalito. The sight of the Golden Gate Bridge sparked her to flick in at various booths for various views of all the bridges in the Bay Area. For Karin, as for most of humanity, Earth was represented by a small section of the planet.

There had been changes. She got too close to the Bay Bridge and was horrified at the rust. It had never occurred to her that the San Francisco citizenry might let the bridges decay. *Something* could be done with them: line them with shops à la London Bridge, or landscape them over for a park, or run drag races.... They would make horribly obtrusive corpses. They would ruin the scenery. Still, that had happened before....

Some things had not changed. She walked for an hour in King's Free Park, the landscaped section of what had been the

San Diego Freeway. The trees had grown a little taller, but the crowds were the same, always different yet always the same. The shops and crowds in the Santa Monica Mall hadn't changed . . . except that the city had filled in the space between the curbs, where people had to step down into the empty streets.

She did some shopping in the Mall. To a saleslady in Magnin's West she said, "Dress me." That turned out to be a considerable project, and it cost. When she left, her new clothes felt odd on her, but they seemed to blend better with the crowds around her.

She did a lot of flicking around without ever leaving the booth—the ubiquitous booth that seemed to be one instead of millions, that seemed to move with her as she explored. It took her longer to find the right numbers than it did to dial. But she flicked down the length of Wilshire Boulevard in jumps of four blocks, from the coast to Central Los Angeles, by simply dialing four digits higher each time.

She stopped off at the Country Art Museum in Fresno and was intrigued by giant sculptures in plastic foam. She was wandering through these shapes, just feeling them, not yet trying to decide whether she liked them, when her wrist phone rang.

She could have taken the call then and there, but she went to a wall phone in the lobby. Karin preferred to see who she was talking to.

She recognized him at once.

Robin Whyte was a round old man, his face pink and soft and cherubic, his scalp bare but for a fringe of white hair over his ears and a single tuft at the top of his head. Karin was surprised to see him now. He was the last living member of the team that had first demonstrated teleportation in 1992. He had been president of JumpShift, Inc., for several decades, but he had retired just after the launching of *Lazarus II*.

"Karin Sagan?" His frown gave him an almost petulant look. "My congratulations on your safe return."

"Thank you." Karin's smile was sunny. An impulse made her add, "Congratulations to you, too."

He did not respond in kind. "I need to see you. Urgently. Can you come immediately?"

"Concerning what?"

"Concerning the interview you gave this morning."

But the interview had gone so well. What could be bothering the man? She said, "All right."

The number he gave her had a New York prefix.

It was evening in New York City. Whyte's apartment was the penthouse floor of a half-empty building. The city itself had lost half its population during the last forty years, and it showed in the walls of dark windows visible through Whyte's picture windows.

"The thing I want to emphasize," said Whyte, "is that I didn't call you here as a representative of JumpShift. I'm retired. But I've got a problem, and pretty quick I'm going to have to take it up with someone in JumpShift. I still own enough JumpShift stock to want to protect it."

His guests made no comment on his disclaimer. They watched as he finished making their drinks and served them. Karin Sagan was curious and a bit truculent at being summoned so abruptly. Jerryberry Jansen had known Whyte too long for that. He was only curious.

"You've put JumpShift in a sticky situation," said Whyte. "Both of you, and the rest of the news media too. Karin, Jerryberry, how do you feel about the space program?"

"I'm for it. You know that," said Jerryberry.

"I'm in it," said Karin. "I feel no strong urge to quit and get an honest job. Is this a preliminary to firing me?"

"No. I do want to know why you went into to so much detail on *Lazarus.*"

"They asked me. If someone had asked me to keep my mouth shut on the subject I might have. Might not."

"We can't rescue *Lazarus,*" said Whyte.

There was an uncomfortable silence. Perhaps it was in both their minds, but it was Jerryberry who said it. "Can't or won't?"

"How long have you known me?"

Jerryberry stopped to count. "Fourteen years, on and off. Look, I'm not saying you'd leave a six-man crew in the lurch if it were feasible to rescue them. But is it *economically* infeasible? Is that it?"

"No. It's impossible." Whyte glared at Karin, who glared back. "You should have figured it out, even if he didn't." He transferred the glare to Jansen. "About that rescue mission you proposed on nationwide teevee. Did you have any details worked out?"

Jerryberry sipped at his Screwdriver. "I'd think it would be obvious. Send a rescue ship. Our ships are infinitely better than anything they had in 2004."

"They're moving at a seventh of lightspeed. What kind of ship could get up the velocity to catch *Lazarus* and still get back?"

"A drop ship, of course! A drop ship burns all its fuel getting up to speed. *Lazarus II* is doing a third of lightspeed, and it cost about a quarter of what *Lazarus* cost—it's so much simpler. You send a drop ship, When it passes *Lazarus* you drop a rescue ship through."

"Uh huh. And how fast is the rescue ship moving?"

"...Oh." *Lazarus* would flash past the rescue ship at a seventh of lightspeed.

"We've got better ships than the best they could do in 2004. Sure we do. But, censored dammit, they don't travel the same way!"

"Well, yes, but there's got to be—"

"You're cheating a little," Karin said. "A rescue ship of the *Lazarus* type could get up to speed and still have the fuel to get home. Meanwhile you send a drop ship to intercept *Lazarus.* The rescue ship drops through the receiver cage, picks them up—hmm."

"It would have to be self-teleporting, wouldn't it? Like *Phoenix.*"

"Yah. Hmmm."

"If you put a transmitter hull around something the size of *Lazarus,* fuel tanks included, you'd pretty near double the weight. It couldn't get up to speed and then decelerate afterward. You'd need more fuel, more weight, a bigger hull. Maybe it couldn't be done at all, but sure as hell we're talking about something a lot bigger than *Lazarus.*"

There had never been another ship as big as *Lazarus.*

Karin said, "Yah. You'd ditch a lot of fuel tanks getting up to speed, but still—hmm. Fuel to get home. Dammit, Whyte, I left Earth nine years ago. You've had nine years to improve the space industry! What have you done?

"We've got lots better drop ships," Why said quietly. Then,

"Don't you understand? We're improving our ships, but not in the direction of a bigger and better *Lazarus*."

Silence.

"Then there's the drop ship itself. We've never built a receiver cage big enough to take another *Lazarus*. *Phoenix* isn't big, it doesn't have to go anywhere. I won't swear it's impossible to build a drop ship that size, but I wouldn't doubt it either. It doesn't matter. We can't build a rescue ship. We don't even have the technology to build *Lazarus* again! It's gone, junked when we started building drop ships!"

"Like those damn big bridges in San Francisco Bay," whispered Karin. "Sorry, gentlemen. I hadn't thought it out."

Jerryberry said, "You've still got the Corliss accelerator. And we still use reaction drives."

"Sure. For interplanetary speeds. And drop ships."

Jerryberry drained his Screwdriver in three swallows. With his mind's eye he saw six coffins, deathly still, and six human beings frozen inside. Three men, three women. Someone must have thought that a scout crew might just decide to colonize the Centaurus system without waiting. Fat chance of that now. Three men, three women, frozen, falling through interplanetary space forever. They couldn't possibly have been expecting rescue. Could they?

"So we don't get them back," he said. "What are we holding, a wake?"

"They knew the risks they were taking," said Whyte. "They knew, and they fought for the chance. We had over a thousand volunteers at the start of training, and that was after the preliminary weeding-out. Jerryberry, I asked you before about how you felt about the space program."

"I told you. In fact—" He stopped. "Publicity."

"Right."

"I thought I was doing you some good. Public support for the space program isn't heavy right now, and frankly, Doctor Sagan, your report didn't help much."

She flared up. "What were we supposed to do, *build* a planet?"

"Failure of the first expedition. No planets. A whole colony fleet on its way home without ever having so much as *seen* Alpha Centaurus! I know, it's safer for them, and better not to waste the time, but dammit!" Jerryberry was on his feet and pacing. There was an odd glow in his eyes, an intensity that could communicate even through a teevee screen. "I tried to emphasize the good points. Now—I damn near promised the world a rescue mission, didn't I?"

"Just about. You weren't the only one."

He paced. "I'm pretty good at explaining. I have to be. I'll just have to tell them—no, let's do it right. Robin, will you go on teevee?"

Whyte looked startled.

"Tell you what," said Jerryberry. "Don't just tell them why we can't rescue *Lazarus.* Show them. Set up a cost breakdown, in dollars and years. We all know—"

"I tell you it isn't *cost.* It—"

"We both know that it *could* be done, if we gave up the rest of the space industry and concentrated solely on rescuing *Lazarus* for enough years. R and D, rebuilding old hardware—"

"Censored dammit! The research alone on a drop ship that size—" Whyte cocked his head as if listening to an inner voice. "That is one way to put it. It would cost us everything we've built up in the past thirty years. Jerryberry, is this really the way to get it across?"

"I don't know. It's one way. Set up a cost estimate you can defend. It won't end with just one broadcast. You'll be challenged, whatever you say. Can you be ready in two days?"

Karin gave a short, barking laugh.

Whyte smiled indulgently. "Are you out of your mind? A valid cost estimate would take months, assuming I can get anyone interested in doing a cost estimate of something nobody really wants built."

Jerryberry paced. "Suppose *we* do a cost estimate, CBA, I mean. Then you wouldn't have anything to defend. It wouldn't be very accurate, but I'm sure we could get within a factor of two."

"Better give yourselves a week. I'll give you the names of some people at JumpShift; you can go to them for details. Meanwhile I'll have them issue a press release saying we're not planning a rescue mission for *Lazarus* at this time."

JumpShift Experimental Laboratory, Building One, was a tremendous pressurized Quonset hut. On most of his previous visits Jerryberry had found it nearly empty; too many of JumpShift's projects are secret. Once he had come here with a camera team, and on that occasion the polished, smoothly curved hull of *Phoenix* had nearly filled the building.

He had never known exactly where the laboratory was. Its summers and winters matched the Northern Hemisphere, and the sun beyond the windows now stood near noon, which put it on Rocky Mountain time.

Gemini Jones was JumpShift's senior research physicist, an improbably tall and slender black woman made even taller by a head of hair like a great white dandelion. "We get this free," she said, rapping the schematic diagrams spread across the table. "The Corliss accelerator. Robin wants to build another of these. We don't have the money yet. Anyway, we can use it for the initial boost. "

On a flattish disk of asteroidal rock a mile across, engineers of the past generation had raised a tower of metal rings. The electromagnetic cannon had been firing ships from Earth orbit since AD 2004. Today it was used more than ever, to accelerate the self-transmitting ships partway toward the orbital velocities of Mars, Jupiter, Mercury. . . .

Jerryberry studied the tower of rings, wider than any ship ever built. "Is it wide enough for what we've got in mind?"

"I think so. We'd fire the rescue ship in sections, then put it together in space. But we'd still have to put a transmitter hull around it."

"Okay, we've got the accelerator, and we'd use standard tanks. Beyond that—"

"Now hold up," said Gem. "There's an easier way to do this. I thought of it this morning. If we do it my way we won't need any research at all."

"Oh? You interest me strangely."

"See, we've still got this problem of building a ship big enough to make the rescue and then decelerate, and a drop cage big enough to take it. But we already know we can build self-transmitting hulls the size of *Phoenix*. What we can do is put the deceleration fuel in *Phoenix* hulls. We wouldn't need an unreasonably big drop cage that way."

Jerryberry whistled. He knew what *Phoenix* had cost. Putting a rescue ship together would be like building a fleet of *Phoenixes.* And yet—

"Robin was wrong. We could *do* that. We've got the hardware."

"That's exactly right. I figure maybe twenty *Phoenix* hulls full of slurried hydrogen, plus a *Phoenix*-type ship for the rescue, plus a couple more hulls to hold the drive and the rigging to string it all together. You'd have to assemble it after launch and accelerate it to a seventh of lightspeed, using a couple hundred standard tanks. Then take it apart, stow the rigging, and send everything through a Lazarus II drop ship one hull at a time."

"We could *do* it. Does Robin know about this?"

"Who's had time to call him? I only just thought of this an hour ago. I've been working on the math."

"We could do it." Jerryberry said, his eyes afire. "We could bring 'em back. All it would take would be time and money."

She smiled indulgently down at him; at least she always seemed to, though her eyes were level with his own. "Don't get too involved. Who's going to pay for all this? You might talk your bemused public into it if you were extending man's dominion across the stars. But to rescue six failures?"

"You don't really think of them that way."

"Nope. But somebody's going to say it."

"I don't know. Maybe we should go for it. Those self-transmitting hulls could be turned into ships afterward."

"No. You'd drop them on the way back."

Jerryberry ran a hand through his hair. "I guess you're

right. Thanks, Gem. You've done a lot of work for something that isn't ever going to get built."

"Good practice. Keeps my brain in shape," said Gem.

He was at home, doggedly working out a time-and-costs schedule for the rescue of *Lazarus*, when Karin Sagan called. She said, "I've been wondering if you need me for the broadcast."

"Good idea," said Jerryberry, "if you're willing. We could tape an interview any time you're ready. I'll ask you to describe the circumstances under which you found *Lazarus*, and use that to introduce the topic."

"Good."

Jerryberry was tired and depressed. It took him a moment to see that Karin was too. "What's wrong?"

"Oh . . . a lot of things. We aren't just going to forget about those six astronauts, are we?"

His laugh was brittle. "I think it unlikely. They aren't decently dead. They're in limbo, falling across our sky forever."

"That's what I mean. We could wake them any time in the next thousand years, if we could get to them."

"That's my problem. We can."

"What?"

"But it'd cost the Moon, so to speak. Come on over, Doctor. I'll show you."

Lazarus cost	N$2,000,000,000
Lazarus II cost	N$ 500,000,000
Phoenix cost	N$ 10,000,000
Colony (six ships adequately equipped) cost	N$ 660,000,000
Support systems in solar system	N$ 250,000,000

Total colony package, including colony and *Phoenix* and support systems in solar system:	N$1,520,000,000
Twenty-two self-transmitting hulls cost (one self-transmitting hull costs N$70,000,000):	N$1,540,000,000
Interstellar drop ship costs	N$ 500,000,000
Phoenix-type rescue ship costs	N$ 110,000,000
R & D costs nothing	
Support systems in solar system	N$ 250,000,000
Total cost of rescue	N$2,300,000,000

"... which is just comfortably more than it cost to build *Lazarus* in the first place, and a lot more than it cost us to not colonize Alpha Centarus. It wouldn't be impossible to go get them. Just inconvenient and expensive."

"In spades," said Karin. "You'd tie up the Corliss accelerator for a week solid. The whole trip would take about thirty-four years starting from the launching of the drop ship."

"And if it could be done now it could always be done; we couldn't ever forget it until we'd done it. And it would get more difficult every year because *Lazarus* would be getting further away."

"It'll nag us the rest of our lives." Karin leaned back in Jerryberry's guest chair. His apartment was not big: three rooms, with doors knocked between them, in a complex that had been a motel on the Pacific Coast Highway thirty years ago. "There's another thing. What are we really doing if we do it Whyte's way? We're talking the public into not backing a space project. Suppose they got the habit? I don't know about you—"

"I just plain like rocket ships," said Jerryberry.

"Okay. Can you really talk the public into this?"

"No. *Lazarus* didn't even cost this much, and *Lazarus* almost didn't get built, they tell me. And *Lazarus* failed, and so did the colony project. So: no. But I'm not sure I can bring myself to talk them out of it."

"Jansen, just how bad is public support for the Space Authority?"

"Oh . . . it isn't even that, exactly. The public is getting unhappy about JumpShift itself."

"What? What for?"

"CBA runs a continuous string of public opinion polls. The displacement booths did genuinely bring some unique problems with them—"

"They solved some too. Maybe you don't remember."

Jerryberry smiled. "I'm not old enough. Neither are you. Slums, traffic jams, plane crashes—nobody's that old except Robin Whyte, and if you try to tell him the booths brought problems of their own, he thinks you're an ungrateful bastard. But they did. You know they did."

"Like flash crowds?"

"Sure. Any time anything interesting happens anywhere, some newstaper is going to report it. Then people flick in to see it from all over the United States. If it gets big enough you get people flicking in just to see the crowd, plus pickpockets, looters, cops, more newstapers, anyone looking for publicity.

"Then there's the drug problem. There's no way to stop smuggling. You can pick a point in the South Pacific with the same longitude and opposite latitude as any given point in the USA and most of Canada, and teleport them from there without worrying about the Earth's rotational velocity. All it takes is two booths. You can't stop the drugs from coming in. I remember one narcotics cop telling me to think of it as evolution in action."

"God."

"Oh, and the ecologists don't like the booths. They make wilderness areas too available. And the cops have their problems. A man used to be off the hook if he could prove he was somewhere else when a crime happened. These days you have to suspect anyone, anywhere. The real killer gets lost in the crowd.

"But the real beef is something else. There are people you have to get along with, right?"

"Not me," said Karin.

"Well, you're unusual. Everyone in the world lives next door to his boss, his mother-in-law, the girl he's trying to drop, the guy he's fighting for a promotion. You *can't move away* from anyone. It bugs people."

"What can they do? Give up the booths?"

"No. There aren't any more cars or planes or railroads. But they can give up space."

Karin thought about that. Presently she gave her considered opinion. "Idiots."

"No. They're just like all of us: They want something for nothing. Have you ever solved a problem without finding another problem just behind it?"

"Sure. My husband ... well, no, I was pretty lonely after we split up. But I didn't sit down and cry about it. When someone hands me a problem, I solve it. Jansen, we're going at this wrong. I feel it."

"Okay, so we're doing it wrong. What's the right way?"

"I don't know. We've got better ships than anyone dreamed of in 2004. That's fact."

"Define *ship*."

"Ship! Vehicle! Never mind, I see the point. Don't push it."

So he didn't ask her what a 747 circling the sinking *Titanic* could have done to help, or whether a Greyhound bus could have crossed the continent in 1849. He said. "We know how to rescue *Lazarus.* What's the big decision. We do or we don't."

"Well?"

"I don't know. We watch the opinion polls. I think . . . I think we'll wind up neutral. Present the project as best we can finagle it up. Tell 'em the easiest way to do it, tell 'em what it'll cost, and leave it at that."

The opinion polls were a sophisticated way to read mass minds. Over the years sampling techniques had improved enormously, raising their accuracy and lowering their cost. Public thinking generally came in blocks.

JumpShift's news release provoked no immediate waves. But one block of thinking began to surface. A significant segment of humanity was old enough to have watched teevee coverage of the launching of *Lazarus.* A smaller, still significant segment had helped pay for it with their taxes.

It had been the most expensive space project of all time. *Lazarus* had been loved. Nothing but love could have pushed the taxpayer into paying such a price. Even those who had fought the program thirty-one years ago now remembered *Lazarus* with love.

The reaction came mainly from older men and women, but it was worldwide. *Save Lazarus.*

Likewise there were those dedicated to saving the ecology from the intrusion of Man. For them the battle was never-ending. True, industrial wastes were no longer dumped into the air and water; the worst of these were flicked through a drop ship into close orbit around Venus, to disappear into the atmosphere of that otherwise useless world. But the ultimate garbage-maker was himself the most dangerous of threats. Hardly a wilderness was left on Earth that was not being settled by men with JumpShift booths.

They would have fought JumpShift on any level. JumpShift proposed to leave three men and three women falling across the sky forever. To hell with their profit margin: save *Lazarus.*

There were groups who would vote against anything done in space. The returns from space exploration had been great, admittedly, but they all derived from satellites in close orbit around Earth: observatories, weather satellites, teevee transmitters, solar power plants. These were dirt cheap these days, and their utility had surely been obvious to any moron since Neanderthal times.

But what use were the worlds of other stars? Even the worlds of the solar system had given no benefit to Man, except for Venus, which made an excellent garbage dump. Better to spend the money on Earth. *Abandon Lazarus.*

But most of the public voted a straight *Insufficient Data.* And of course they were right.

Robin Whyte was nervous. He was trying not to show it, but he paced too much and he smiled too much and he kept clasping his hands behind his back. "Sit down, for Christ's sake," said Jerryberry. "Relax. They can't throw tomatoes through their teevee screens."

Whyte laughed. "We're working on that in the research division. Are you almost ready?"

"An hour to broadcast. I've already done the interview with Doctor Sagan. It's on tape."

"Let's see what you've got."

What CBA had for this broadcast was a fully detailed rescue project, complete with artist's conceptions. Jerryberry spread the paintings along a wall. "Using your artists, whom we hired for a week with JumpShift's kind permission. Aren't they beautiful? We also have a definite price tag. Two billion three hundred million new dollars."

Whyte's laugh was still shaky. "That's right on the borderline. Barely feasible." He was looking at an artist's conception of the launching of the rescue mission: a stream of spherical fuel tanks and larger, shark-shaped *Phoenix* hulls pouring up through the ringed tower of the Corliss accelerator. More components rested on flat rock at the launch end. "So Gem thought of it first. I must be getting old."

"You don't expect to think of everything do you? You once told me that your secretary thought of the fresh-water tower gimmick during a drunken office party."

"True, too. I paid her salary for thirty years, hoping she'd do it again, but she never did.... Do you think they'll buy it?"

"No."

"I guess not." Whyte seemed to shake himself. "Well, maybe we'll use it some other time. It's a useful technique, shipping fuel in *Phoenix* hulls. We'll probably need it to explore, say, Barnard's Star, which is moving pretty censored fast with respect to Sol."

"We don't have to tell them they can't do it. Just tell 'em the price tag and let them make up their own minds."

"Listen, I had a hand in launching *Lazarus.* The launching boosters were fueled by JumpShift units."

"I know."

Whyte, prowling restlessly, was back in front of the launching scene. "I always thought they should have drilled right through the asteroid. Leave the Corliss accelerator open at both ends."

Activity in the sound studio had diminished. Against a white wall men had placed a small table and two chairs, and a battery of teevee cameras and lights were aiming their muzzles into the scene.

Jerryberry touched Whyte's arm. "Let's go sit down over there." Whyte might freeze up if confronted by the cameras too suddenly. Give him a chance to get used to it.

Whyte didn't move. His head was cocked to one side, and his lips moved silently.

"What's the matter?"

Whyte made a shushing motion.

Jerryberry waited.

Presently Whyte looked up. "You'll have to scrap this. How much time have we got?"

"But—An hour. Less. What do you mean, scrap it?"

Whyte smiled. "I just thought of something. Get me to a telephone, will you? Has Gem still got the schematics of the Corliss accelerator?

An hour to broadcast time, and Jerryberry began to shake. "Robin, are we going to have a broadcast or not?"

Whyte patted him on the arm. "Count on it."

Gem Jones's big white-on-blue schematic had been thumbtacked to the white wall over the table and chairs. Below it, Jerryberry Jansen leaned back, seemingly relaxed, watching Whyte move about with a piece of chalk.

A thumbtacked blueprint and a piece of chalk. It was slipshod by professional standards. Robin Whyte had not appeared on teevee in a couple of decades. He made professional mistakes: he turned his back on the audience, he covered what he was drawing with the chalk. But he didn't look nervous. He grinned into the cameras as if he could see old friends out there.

"The heart of it is the Corliss accelerator," he said, and with the chalk he drew an arc underneath the tower's launch cradle, through the rock itself. "We excavate here, carve out a space to get the room. Then—" He drew it in.

A JumpShift drop ship receiver cage.

"The rescue ship is self-transmitting, of course. As it leaves the accelerator it transmits back to the launch end. What we have then is an electromagnetic cannon of infinite length. We spin it on its axis so it doesn't get out of alignment. We give the ship an acceleration of one gee for a bit less than two months to boost it to the velocity of *Lazarus*, then we flick it out to the drop ship.

"This turns out to be a relatively cheap operation," Whyte said. "We could put some extra couches in *Phoenix* and use that. We could even use the accelerator to boost the drop ship up to speed, but that would take four months, and we'd have to do it *now*. It would mean building another Corliss accelerator, but—" Whyte grinned into the cameras "—we should have done that anyway, years ago. There's enough traffic to justify it.

"Return voyage is just as simple. After they pick up the crew of *Lazarus*, they flick to the Pluto drop ship, which is big enough to catch them, then to the Mercury drop ship to lose their potential energy, then back to the Corliss accelerator drop cage. We use the accelerator for another two months to slow it down. The cost of an interstellar drop ship is half a billion new dollars. A new Corliss accelerator would cost us about the same, and we can use it commercially. Total price is half of what *Lazarus* cost." Whyte put down the chalk and sat.

Jerryberry said, "When can you go ahead with this, Doctor?"

"JumpShift will submit a time-and-costs schedule to the UN Space Authority. I expect it'll go to the world vote."

"Thank you, Doctor Whyte, for..." It was a formula. When the cameras were off Jerryberry sagged in his chair. "Now I can say it. Boy, are you out of practice."

"What do you mean? Didn't I get it across?"

"I think you did. I hope so. You smiled a lot too much. On camera that makes you look self-satisfied."

"I know, you told me before," said Whyte. "I couldn't help it. I just felt so *good*."

BIBLIOGRAPHY

OPUS NO. | TITLE AND PUBLISHING HISTORY

1. "The Coldest Place," *Worlds of If*, December 1964
   Collection, *Tales of Known Space* (#84)
2. "World of Ptavvs," novella, *Worlds of Tomorrow*, March 1965
   Expanded to novel length, 1966, see #10
3. "Wrong Way Street," *Galaxy*, April 1965
   The Ninth Galaxy Reader, ed. Frederik Pohl, 1966
   Anthology, *Voyagers in Time*, ed. Robert Silverberg, 1967
   Anthology, *First Flights to the Moon*, ed. Hal Clement, 1970
   Collection, *Convergent Series* (#113)
   Portuguese anthology, *Viajantes No Tempo*, Galleria Panorama, as "Rua de Sentido Unico"
   German anthology, *Die Morder Mohameds*, Marion von Schroder Verlag, 1970, as "Falsche Richtung"
   Dutch anthology, *Alfa Een*, Meulenhoff Nederland B.V., 1973, as "Tweerichtingsverkeer"
4. "One Face," *Galaxy*, June 1965
   Collection, *The Shape of Space* (#40)
   Collection, *Inconstant Moon* (#60)
   Collection, *Convergent Series* (#113)
   Galaxie (France), Juin 1967
   Dutch anthology, *Science Fiction-Verhalen*, Amsterdam: Meulenhoff, as "De Schaduzijde"
5. "Becalmed in Hell," *Fantasy and Science Fiction (F&SF)*, July 1965
   Anthology, *World's Best Science Fiction: 1966*, ed. Donald A. Wollheim and Terry Carr, 1966
   Anthology, *Nebula Award Stories*, ed. Damon Knight, 1966
   Anthology, *Twenty Years of* F&SF, ed. Edward L. Ferman and Robert P. Mills, 1970

Collection, *All The Myriad Ways* (#54)
Collection, *Inconstant Moon* (#60)
Collection, *Tales of Known Space* (#84)
Dutch anthology, *De Speekselboom*, ed. Damon Knight *(Nebula Award Stories 1)* as "Dobberen in de hel"
German anthology, *Der Gigant*, Science-Fiction-Erzahlungen, as "Panne in der Holle"
Collection, *Playgrounds of the Mind* (#178)

6. "The Warriors," *Worlds of If*, February 1966
Collection, *The Shape of Space* (#40)
Collection, *Tales of Known Space* (#84)
Anthology, *The Man-Kzin Wars*, ed. Larry Niven, 1988

7. "Eye of an Octopus," *Galaxy*, February 1966
Collection, *Tales of Known Space* (#84)

8. "Bordered in Black," *F&SF*, April 1966
Collection, *The Shape of Space* (#40)
Collection, *Inconstant Moon* (#60)
Anthology, *SF: Author's Choice 3*, ed. Harry Harrison
Collection, *Convergent Series* (#113)
Collection, *N-Space* (#177A)

9. "By Mind Alone," *Worlds of If*, June 1966

10. *World of Ptavvs*, Ballantine, 1966
also MacDonald, Sphere
French edition: *Le Monde de Ptavvs*, Editions Opta, 1974
Dutch edition: *Kzanol The Ruimtepiraat*, Prisma, Het Nederlandse Pocketboek, © 1970, Het Spectrum
Spanish edition: *El Mundo De Los Ptavvs*, Madrid: Edaf, 1976
German edition: *Das Doppelhirn*, Bastei Lubbe, 1977
Italian edition: *Stasi Interrotta*, Fanucci Editore, 1976
Dutch edition: *De Wereld Van De Ptavvs*, Amsterdam/Brussel: Elsevier SF, Nederland B.V., 1979

11. "How the Heroes Die," *Galaxy*, October 1966
Collection, *The Shape of Space* (#40)
Collection, *Inconstant Moon* (#60)
Collection, *Tales of Known Space* (#84)

12. "Neutron Star," *Worlds of If*, October 1966
Collection, *Neutron Star* (#26)
Anthology, *Where Do We Go From Here?* ed. Isaac Asimov, 1971
Anthology, *The Hugo Winners*, volume 2, ed. Isaac Asimov, 1971
Anthology, *The Arbor House Treasury of Modern Science Fiction*, ed. Robert Silverberg and Martin H. Greenberg, 1980
Galaxie Mars 1968 (France), as "L'Etoile Invisible"
Galactica (Hungary)
Collection, *Worlds of If: A Retrospective Anthology*, ed. Frederik Pohl, Martin H. Greenberg, Joseph D. Olander, 1986
Anthology, *The Super Hugos*, presented by Isaac Asimov, 1992

13. "At the Core," *Worlds of If*, November 1966
Anthology, *The Second If Reader of Science Fiction*, ed. Frederik Pohl, 1968
Collection, *Neutron Star* (#26)
Galaxie (France), Avril 1968, as "Jusqu'au Coeur"

14. "At the Bottom of a Hole," *Galaxy*, December 1966
Collection, *The Shape of Space* (#40)
Collection, *Inconstant Moon* (#60)
Collection, *Tales of Known Space* (#84)

15. "A Relic of Empire," *Worlds of If*, December 1966
Collection, *Neutron Star* (#26)
Anthology, *The Great Science Fiction Series*, with commentary, 1980
Galactica (Hungary)
Collection, *Playgrounds of the Mind* (#178)

16. "The Soft Weapon," *Worlds of If*, February 1967
    Collection, *Neutron Star* (#26)
    Galaxie (France), Septembre 1971, as "L'Arme Molle"
    Collection, *Playgrounds of the Mind* (#178)
17. "The Long Night," *F&SF*, March 1967
    Collection, *Inconstant Moon* (#60) as "Convergent Series"
    Collection, *Convergent Series* (#113) as "Convergent Series"
    Anthology, *Mathenauts*, ed. Rudy Rucker, 1987, as "Convergent Series"
    Collection, *N-Space* (#177A) as "Convergent Series"
18. "Flatlander," *Worlds of If*, March 1967
    Collection, *Neutron Star* (#26)
    Anthology, *Seven Trips Through Time And Space*, ed. Groff Conklin, 1968
19. "The Ethics of Madness," *Worlds of If*, April 1967
    Collection, *Neutron Star* (#26)
20. "Safe at Any Speed," *F&SF*, May 1967
    Collection, *The Shape of Space* (#40)
    Collection, *Tales of Known Space* (#84)
    Anthology, *One Hundred Great Science Fiction Short Short Stories*, ed. Isaac Asimov, Martin H. Greenberg, and Joseph D. Olander, 1978
21. "The Adults," *Galaxy*, June 1967
22. "The Jigsaw Man," anthology, *Dangerous Visions*, ed. Harlan Ellison, Doubleday, 1967
    Berkley, Sphere, Signet
    Collection, *All The Myriad Ways* (#54)
    Collection, *Tales of Known Space* (#84)
    Anthology, *The Road to Science Fiction #3*, ed. James Gunn, 1979
    French anthology, *Dangereuses Visions*, J'ai Lu, 1967

23. "The Handicapped," *Galaxy*, December 1967
Collection, *Neutron Star* (#26) as "Handicap"
Anthology, *World's Best Science Fiction 1968*, ed. Donald A. Wollheim and Terry Carr, as "Handicap"

24. *Slowboat Cargo*, serial, *Galaxy*, February, March, and April 1968
In book form as *A Gift from Earth* (#34)

25. "The Deceivers," *Galaxy*, April 1968
Collection, *Tales of Known Space* (#84) as "Intent to Deceive"
German anthology, *Galaxy 13*, Munich: Wilhelm Heyne Verlag as "Bedienung Inbegriffen," 1969

26. *Neutron Star*, collection, Ballantine
MacDonald 1969, Sphere
Urania (Italy), as "Reliquia Dell'imperio"
German edition: Wilhelm Goldmann Verlag

27. "Grendel," *Neutron Star* (#26)

28. "Dry Run," *F&SF*, May 1968
Collection, *The Shape of Space* (#40)
Collection, *Convergent Series* (#113)
Magazine de Ficcao Cientifica (Portugal), Julho 1971, as "Tentativa Simulada"

29. "The Deadlier Weapon," *Ellery Queen's Mystery Magazine*, June 1968
Collection, *The Shape of Space* (#40)
Collection, *Inconstant Moon* (#60)
Collection, *Convergent Series* (#113)

30. "There Is a Tide," *Galaxy*, June 1968
Collection, *A Hole In Space* (#74)
Collection, *Tales of Known Space* (#84)
Het Heelal Van Der Dromers (Netherlands), as "Er Is Een Getij"
German anthology, *Galaxy 12*, Munich: Wilhelm Heyne Verlag, 1969, as "Das Glucksspiel"

31. "Wait It Out," *Future Unbounded*, Program Book for FUnCon, 1968
    Anthology, *Tomorrow's Worlds* (revised), ed. Robert Silverberg
    Collection, *All The Myriad Ways* (#54)
    Collection, *Tales of Known Space* (#84)
    Collection, *Inconstant Moon* (#60)
    Collection, *Playgrounds of the Mind* (#178)
32. "For a Foggy Night"
    Decal (fanzine), ed. Donald Cochrane, July 1968
    Collection, *All The Myriad Ways* (#54)
    Collection, *N-Space* (#177A)
33. "Like Banquo's Ghost," *Worlds of If*, September 1968
    Collection, *The Shape of Space* (#40)
    Alternities (semiprozine), Autumn/Winter 1980
    Collection, *Convergent Series* (#113)
34. *A Gift From Earth*, Ballantine, 1968
    British edition: MacDonald 1969, SFBC 1969, Sphere
    Hardcover edition, Walker (USA), 1970
    German edition: *Planet Der Verlornen*, Bastei Lubbe, 1972 & 1982
    Italian edition: *Un Dono Dalla Terra*, Futuro, 1973
    Netherlands edition: *Een Geschenk Van De Arrde*, Amsterdam: Meulenhoff, 1976
    Japanese edition: Hayakawa Publishing, Inc., 1979
35. "The Meddler," *F&SF*, October 1968
    Collection, *The Shape of Space* (#40)
    Collection, *Convergent Series* (#113)
    Collection, *N-Space* (#177A)
36. "All The Myriad Ways," *Galaxy*, October 1968
    Anthology, *Worlds of Maybe*, ed. Robert Silverberg
    Collection, *All The Myriad Ways* (#54)

Graphic version, *Psycho*, November 1972, as "All the Ways and Means to Die"
Anthology, *Galaxy: Thirty Years of Innovative Science Fiction*, with memoir, Playboy Press, 1980
Collection, *N-Space* (#177A)

37. "The Organleggers," *Galaxy*, January 1969
Collection, *The Shape of Space* (#40) as "Death by Ecstasy"
Collection, *The Long Arm of Gil Hamilton* (#88), as "Death by Ecstasy"

38. "The Theory and Practice of Teleportation," *Galaxy*, March 1969
Collection, *All The Myriad Ways* (#54), as "Exercise in Speculation: The Theory and Practice of Teleportation"

39. "Not Long Before the End," *F&SF*, April 1969
Anthology, *Nebula Award Stories #5*, ed. James Blish, 1970
Collection, *All The Myriad Ways* (#54)
Collection, *Inconstant Moon* (#60)
Anthology, *The Golden Road*, ed. Damon Knight, 1973
Graphic edition, *Unknown Worlds of Science Fiction*, May 1975
Anthology, *The Magic May Return*, ed. Larry Niven (#127)
Collection, *The Time of the Warlock*, illustrated by Dennis Wolf (#154)

40. *The Shape of Space*, collection, Ballantine, 1969
German edition; Wilhelm Goldmann Verlag, as *Letztes Signal Von Alpha Centauri*

41. "Man of Steel/Woman of Kleenex," *Knight*, December 1969
Ad Astra #3 (Britain), newszine
Graphic underground, dramatized, *More Existentialist Fun Comics #2*
Anthology, *Superheroes*, ed. Michael Perry
Hayne Science Fiction Magazine 12
Anthology, *Alien Sex*, ed. Ellen Datlow, Dutton
Collection, *N-Space* (#177A)

42. "Passerby," *Galaxy*, September 1969
    Collection, *All The Myriad Ways* (#54)
    Collection, *Inconstant Moon* (#60)
    Collection, *N-Space* (#177A)
43. "Get a Horse!" *F&SF*, October 1969
    Anthology, *The Best From F&SF, #19*, ed. Edward L. Ferman, 1970
    Collection, *The Flight of the Horse* (#64), as "The Flight of the Horse"
    The Saturday Evening Post, June/July 1974
    Graphic edition, *Questar*
    Graphic edition, *Starstream*, ed. Roger Elwood
    Anthology, *Roger Caras' Treasury of Great Horse Stories*, ed. Roger Caras and Martin Greenberg
44. *The Misspelled Magician* with David Gerrold
    Serial, *Worlds of If*, May/June and July/August 1970
    Expanded to *The Flying Sorcerers* (#56)
    Galaxie (France), Mai/Juin 1972, as *Drole de Magicien*
45. "Bird in the Hand," *F&SF*, October 1969
    Anthology, *World's Best Science Fiction 1971*, ed. Donald A. Wollheim and Terry Carr
    Collection, *The Flight of the Horse* (#64)
    Anthology, *Phoenix Feathers*, ed. Barbara Silverberg
46. "Unfinished Story," *F&SF*, December 1970
    Collection, *All The Myriad Ways* (#54), as "Unfinished Story #1"
    American Journal of Physics, February 1975
    Collection, *Playgrounds of the Mind* (#178)
47. "Leviathan!" *Playboy*, August 1970
    Anthology, *Last Train to Limbo*, Playboy Press, 1971
    Collection, *The Flight of the Horse* (#64)
    Anthology, *Seaserpents!* ed. Jack Dann & Gardner Dozois, 1989
    Collection, *Playgrounds of the Mind* (#178)

48. "No Exit," with Henry Stine, *Fantastic*, June 1971

49. "There's a Wolf In My Time Machine," *F&SF*, June 1971
Collection, *The Flight of the Horse* (#64)
Anthology, *Zoo 2000*, ed. Jane Yolen, 1973

50. "The Fourth Profession," *Quark #4*, ed. Samuel R. Delany and Marilyn Hacker
Anthology, *The Best Science Fiction of the Year*, ed. Lester Del Rey, 1973
Anthology, *The 1972 Annual World's Best SF*, ed. Donald A. Wollheim
Collection, *A Hole in Space* (#74)
Sirius (Yugoslavia), broj 61, as "Cetvrta Vjestina"
Anthology, *Project Solar Sail*, ed. Arthur C. Clarke, 1990
Collection, *N-Space* (#177A)

51. "Rammer," *Galaxy*, November 1971
Anthology, *The Best Science Fiction of the Year*, ed. Lester Del Rey, 1972
Anthology, *The Best from Galaxy #1*, no ed. listed, 1972
Collection, *A Hole In Space* (#74)
Included in *World Out Of Time* (#91)
Anthology, *The Best Science Fiction Stories* (no further data)
Science Fiction Story-Reader (Germany), Munich: Wilhelm Heyne Verlag
Collection, *Playgrounds of the Mind* (#178)

52. "What Good is a Glass Dagger?" *F&SF*, September 1971
Collection, *The Flight of the Horse* (#64)
Collection, *Playgrounds of the Mind* (#178)

53. *The Flying Sorcerers* with David Gerrold, Ballantine
German edition: Munich: Wilhelm Heyne Verlag, *Die Fliegenden Zauberer*, 1976 and 1982

54. *All The Myriad Ways*, Ballantine, 1971
German edition: Bastei Lubbe, as *Myriaden*, 1973

Japanese edition, Hayakawa Publishing Inc., 1979

55. "Inconstant Moon" collection, *All The Myriad Ways* (#54)

    Anthology, *Best Science Fiction for 1972*, ed. Frederik Pohl, 1972

    Collection, *Inconstant Moon* (#60)

    Anthology, *The Best of All Possible Worlds*, ed. Spider Robinson, 1980

    German anthology, *Jahresband 1982*, Heyne Science Fiction, Munich: Wilhelm Heyne Verlag, as "Wechselhafter Mond," 1982

    Anthology, *The Hugo Winners #3*, ed. Isaac Asimov, 1977

    Collection, *N-Space* (#177A)

56. "Unfinished Story #2," collection, *All The Myriad Ways* (#54)

57. "What Can You Say About Chocolate Covered Manhole Covers?"

    Collection, *All The Myriad Ways* (#54)

    Collection, *N-Space* (#177A)

58. *Ringworld*, Ballantine, 1970

    British edition: Sphere, Gollancz, 1972

    Holt, Rinehart and Winston, 1977

    Spanish edition: Ediciones Martinez Roca, S.A., as *Mundo Anillo*

    Italian edition: Andromeda (Dell'Oglio), as *Burattinai Nel Cosmo*

    German edition: Bastei Lubbe, as *Ringwelt*

    French edition: Paris: Editions Opta, as *L'Anneau-Monde*, 1973

    Dutch edition: Amsterdam/Brussel: Elsevier Nederland B.V., as *Ringwereld*, 1972, reprinted 1980

    Japanese edition: Hayakawa Publishing, Inc., 1978

    Dutch edition: Meulenhoff SF Fenomeen, as *Ringwereld*, 1989

59. "Flash Crowd," anthology, *Three Trips in Time and Space*, ed. Robert Silverberg, Hawthorne, 1973

    Collection, *The Flight of the Horse* (#64)

60. *Inconstant Moon*, collection, Gollancz, 1973, Sphere, 1974

61. "Cloak of Anarchy," *Analog*, March 1972
Anthology, *Best Science Fiction Stories of the Year #2*, ed. Lester Del Rey
Anthology, *2020 Vision*, ed. Jerry Pournelle, 1974
Collection, *Tales of Known Space* (#84)
Anthology, *Isaac Asimov's Wonderful Worlds of Science Fiction: Tin Stars*, ed. Isaac Asimov, Martin H. Greenberg, & Charles G. Waugh, 1986
Collection, *N-Space* (#177A)

62. "Recipes," *Cooking Out Of This World*, ed. Anne McCaffrey

63. *Protector*, Ballantine, 1973
British edition: Futura Publications
Italian edition: dall' Oglio editore, 1975, as *Il Defensore*
German edition: Wilhelm Goldmann Verlag, as *Der Baum Des Lebens*
French edition: Paris: Editions Albin Michel, 1976, as *Protecteur*
Dutch edition: Elsevier Nederland B.V., 1977, as *Beschermheer*
Japanese edition: Hayakawa Publishing Inc., 1979

64. *The Flight of the Horse*, Ballantine, 1973
British edition: Orbit
Italian edition: Futuro, as *Il Tempo Di Svetz*
Japanese edition: Tokyo: Tokyo Sogensha Company, Ltd.
German edition: Wilhelm Goldmann Verlag, 1981, as *Der Flug Des Pferdes*

65. "Death In a Cage"
Collection, *The Flight of the Horse* (#64)

66. "The Theory and Practice of Time Travel," *Vertex*, April 1973
Anthology, *Looking Ahead: The Vision of Science Fiction*, ed. Dick Allen and Lori Allen, 1975
Collection, *All The Myriad Ways* (#54)

67. "The Alibi Machine," *Vertex*, June 1973
Anthology, *Antigrav: Cosmic Comedies*, ed. Philip Strick, 1976
Collection, *A Hole In Space* (#74)

68. "All the Bridges Rusting," *Vertex*, August 1973
Collection, *A Hole In Space* (#74)

69. "The Defenseless Dead," anthology, *Ten Tomorrows*, ed. Roger Elwood, 1973
Collection, *The Long Arm of Gil Hamilton* (#88)
Collection, *Playgrounds of the Mind* (#178)

70. "The Hole Man," *Analog*, January 1974
Collection, *A Hole In Space* (#74)
Anthology, *The Best Science Fiction of the Year #4*, ed. Terry Carr, 1975
Anthology, *The Hugo Winners #3*, ed. Isaac Asimov, 1977
Anthology, *Black Holes*, ed. Jerry Pournelle, 1978
Sirius (Yugoslavia), broj 143
Anthology, *Science Fiction: Contemporary Mythology: the SFWA-SFRA Anthology*, textbook, with commentary, ed. Patricia S. Warrick, Martin H. Greenberg and Joseph D. Olander
Collection, *N-Space* (#177A)

71. "$16,940.00," *Alfred Hitchcock's Mystery Magazine*, February 1974
Collection, *A Hole In Space* (#74)

72. "Bigger Than Worlds," *Analog*, March 1974, with illustrations by Ames
Speculation (fanzine), as "Alternatives to Worlds"
Collection, *A Hole In Space* (#74)
Anthology, *The Endless Frontier*, ed. Jerry Pournelle, 1979
Collection, *Playgrounds of the Mind*, *Tor*, 1991 (#178)

73. "A Kind of Murder," *Analog*, April 1974
Collection, *A Hole In Space* (#74)
Anthology, *Fear*, Davis Publications, ed. Alfred Hitchcock, 1982

74. *A Hole In Space*, Ballantine, 1974
Orbit
German edition: abridged, Wilhelm Goldmann Verlag, as *De Lucke Im System*

75. "The Last Days of the Permanent Floating Riot Club," collection, *A Hole In Space* (#74)

76. "Plaything," *Worlds of If*, August 1974
Anthology, *The Best from If*, volume 3, ed. James Baen, 1976
Anthology, *100 Great Science Fiction Short Short Stories*, ed. Isaac Asimov, Martin H. Greenberg, and Joseph D. Olander, 1978
Collection, *Convergent Series* (#113)

77. "Night on Mispec Moor," *Vertex*, August 1974
Collection, *Convergent Series* (#113)
Anthology, *Robert Adams' Book of Soldiers*, 1988
Collection, *N-Space* (#177A)

78. *The Mote in God's Eye*, with Jerry Pournelle, Simon & Schuster/Pocket, 1974
British edition: Weidenfeld & Nicholson, Orbit
Japanese edition: Tokyo: Tokyo Sogensha Co. Ltd., 1974
Italian edition: Cosmo, as *La Strada Delle Stelle*
German edition: Munich: Wilhelm Heyne Verlag, 1977, as *De Splitter Im Auge Gottes*
Netherlands edition: Amsterdam: Elsevier, 1978, as *De Splinter in God's Oog*
French edition: Paris: Editions Albin Michel, 1981, as *La Poussiere Dans L'Oeil de Dieu*

79. "The Nonesuch," *F&SF*, December 1974
Collection, *Convergent Series* (#113)

80. "The Borderland of Sol," *Analog*, January 1975
Collection, *Tales of Known Space* (#84)
Anthology, *Black Holes*, ed. Jerry Pournelle, 1978
German anthology, *Im Grenzland Der Sonne*, Munich:

Wilhelm Heyne Verlag
Sirius (Yugoslavia), broj 55, as "Tu Negje Blizu Sola"
Anthology, *The Hugo Winners #4*, 1985, ed. Isaac Asimov
Collection, *Playgrounds of the Mind* (#178)

81. "Singularities Make Me Nervous"
Anthology, *Stellar I*, ed. Judy-Lynn Del Rey, 1974
Collection, *Convergent Series* (#113)
Spain: Loganesi & C., as "Me Cose Strane Mi Innervosiscono"

82. *Inferno*, with Jerry Pournelle, Pocket Books, 1975
British edition: Allen Wingate
Gregg Press
Japanese edition: Tokyo: Tokyo Sogensha Co. Ltd.
Italian edition: Milan: Armenia Editore, 1978, as *Questo E L'Inferno*

83. "Galaxy Stars," (Bio of Jerry Pournelle), *Galaxy*, July 1975

84. *Tales of Known Space*, collection, Ballantine, 1975
Japanese edition: Hayakawa Publishing, Inc.
Spanish edition: Madrid: Edaf, 1978, as *Historias Del Espacio Reconocido*

85. "Timeline for Known Space," "Afterthoughts," and various remarks preceding and following the stories in *Tales of Known Space* (#84)

86. "My Universe and Welcome to It," *Tales of Known Space* (#84)

87. "Arm," *Epoch*, ed. Roger Elwood and Robert Silverberg, 1975
Collection, *The Long Arm of Gil Hamilton* (#88)
Anthology, *The Thirteen Crimes of Science Fiction*, ed. Isaac Asimov, Martin H. Greenberg, and Charles G. Waugh
Sirius (Yugoslavia), broj 136

88. *The Long Arm of Gil Hamilton*, collection, Ballantine, 1976
Dutch edition: Prisma Science Fiction, as *De Lange Arm Van Gil Hamilton*
French edition: Corps 9—Andromede, Maison de la Fiction,

as *Le Troisieme Bras*
Spanish edition: Urania, ed. Arnoldo Mondadori, as *La Terza Mano*

89. "Afterword," *The Long Arm of Gil Hamilton* (#88)
90. *Down in Flames*, outline for a novel, in *Trumpet 9* (fanzine), 1969
On the SF computer networks, 1980s
Collection, *N-Space* (#177A)
91. "Building the Mote in God's Eye," with Jerry Pournelle, *Galaxy*, January 1976
Anthology, *A Step Further Out*, ed. Jerry Pournelle
Collection, *N-Space* (#177A)
92. "Down and Out," *Galaxy*, February 1976
Included in *World Out Of Time* (#91)
Anthology, *The Best from Galaxy #4*, ed. James Baen, 1976
Anthology, *Galaxy: The Best of My Years*, ed. James Baen, 1980
93. "Mistake," anthology, *Stellar #2*, ed. Judy-Lynn Del Rey
Anthology, *One Hundred Great Science Fiction Short Short Stories*, ed. Isaac Asimov, Martin H. Greenberg, and Joseph D. Olander, 1988
Collection, *Convergent Series* (#113)
94. "The Magic Goes Away," novelette, *Odyssey*, Summer 1976
Expanded (#107)
Collection, *The Time of the Warlock*, illustrated by Dennis Wolf (#154)
95. *World Out Of Time*, Holt, Rinehart, Winston, 1976, Ballantine, 1977
Dutch edition: Amsterdam: Deltos Elsevier, as *Buiten De Tijd*
Italian edition: Milan: Editrice Nord, 1977, as *Mondo Senza Tempo*
Brazilian edition: Buenos Aires: 1978, as *Un Mundo Fuera Del Tiemp*
Japanese edition: Hayakawa Publishing Inc., 1979

French edition: Paris: Editions Albin Michel, 1978, as *Un Monde Hors Du Temps*

Israeli edition: paperback, data in Hebrew

96. "Children of the State," serial form of *World Out Of Time*, *Galaxy*, September, October, November 1976

97. "The Words in Science Fiction," anthology, *The Craft of Science Fiction*, ed. Reginald Bretnor, 1976

    Anthology, *Antigrav: Cosmic Comedies*, ed. Philip Strick, 1976

98. *Lucifer's Hammer*, with Jerry Pournelle, Playboy Press, 1977

    Paperback, Fawcett Books, 1978

    British edition: Futura Publications

    Japanese edition: Hayakawa Publishing, Inc.

    German edition: Munich: Wilhelm Heyne Verlag, 1980, as *Luzifers Hammers*

    Belgian edition: A. W. Bruna & Zoon, Utrecht/Antwerpen, 1980, as *De Hamer Van Lucifer*

    Israeli edition: paperback, data in Hebrew

99. "Cruel and Unusual," *Cosmos*, May 1977, as "Three Vignettes"

    Collection, *Convergent Series* (#113)

    Anthology, *Aliens!* ed. Gardner Dozois and Jack M. Dann, as "Four Vignettes," 1980

100. "The Subject is Closed," *Cosmos*, May 1977, as "Three Vignettes"

    Collection, *Convergent Series* (#113)

    Anthology, *Aliens!* ed. Gardner Dozois and Jack M. Dann, as "Four Vignettes," 1982

    Anthology, *Another Round at the Spaceport Bar*, ed. George H. Scithers and Darrell M. Schweitzer, 1989

101. "Grammar Lesson," *Cosmos*, May 1977, as "Three Vignettes"

    Collection, *Convergent Series* (#113)

Anthology, *Aliens!* ed. Gardner Dozois and Jack M. Dann, as "Four Vignettes," 1980

102. "Rotating Cylinders and the Possibility of Global Causality Violation," *Analog*, August 1977

 Collection, *Convergent Series* (#113)

 Isaac Asimov's Science Fiction Magazine (Japanese edition), 1981, along with an extensive interview with photos

103. "The Last Necronomicon," *APA-L #315* (fanzine)

 IS #4 (fanzine)

104. "Cautionary Tales," *Isaac Asimov's Science Fiction Magazine*, July-August 1978

 Collection, *Convergent Series* (#113)

 Anthology, *Isaac Asimov's Science Fiction Anthology*, volume 1, 1978

 Isaac Asimov's Science Fiction Magazine (Japanese edition)

 Collection, *Playgrounds of the Mind* (#178)

105. "Transfer of Power," *Ariel, the Book of Fantasy*, volume 3 (coffee table book), ed. Thomas Durwood, 1978

 Collection, *Convergent Series* (#113)

 Netherlands Anthology, *Nirwana*, Amsterdam: Meulenhoff Nederland B.V., 1981, as "Machtsoverdracht"

106. "Flare Time," anthology, *Andromeda #1*, ed. Peter Weston, 1978

 Amazing Science Fiction Stories, November 1982

 Collection, *Limits* (#151)

 Anthology, *Medea: Harlan's World*, ed. Harlan Ellison, Bantam, 1985

 Collection, *N-Space* (#177A)

107. *The Magic Goes Away*, illustrated novella, Ace Books, 1978

 Japanese edition: Tokyo: Tokyo Sogensha Co. Ltd., illustrations, 1980

 German edition: Bastei Lubbe, illustrations, 1981, as *Wenn Der Zauber Vergeht...*

108. "Assimilating Our Culture, That's What They're Doing!" *Destinies*, November/December 1978, ed. James Baen
Collection, *Convergent Series* (#113)
Anthology, *Aliens!* ed. Gardner Dozois and Jack M. Dann, as "Four Vignettes," 1980
Anthology, *The Best of Destinies*, ed. James Baen, 1980
Collection, *Playgrounds of the Mind* (#178)

109. "The Schumann Computer," *Destinies*, Jan.-Feb. 1979, ed. James Baen
Collection, *Convergent Series* (#113)
French Anthology, *Univers 1980*, as "Le Chirpsithra"

110. "Shall We Indulge in Rishathra?" with cartoons by Bill Rotsler, *Science Fiction Review* (fanzine), March-April 1979
Collection, *N-Space* (#177A)

111. "Spirals," with Jerry Pournelle, *Destinies*, April-June 1979, ed. James Baen
Anthology, *The Endless Frontier*, ed. Jerry Pournelle
Anthology, *The Best of Destinies*, ed. James Baen
Collection, *Limits* (#151)

112. "The Locusts," with Steve Barnes, *Analog*, June 1979
Anthology, *The 1980 Annual World's Best SF*, ed. Donald A. Wollheim
Collection, *Limits* (#151)

113. *Convergent Series*, Ballantine, 1979
British edition: Orbit

114. "Introduction," for *Convergent Series* (#113)

115. "In The Cellar," *Isaac Asimov's Science Fiction Magazine*, Feb. 1979
Isaac Asimov's Science Fiction Magazine (Japanese edition)

116. *The Ringworld Engineers*, serial, *Galileo*, July, September, November 1979, and January 1980
Inbound signatures, limited edition, Phantasia Press

Holt, Rinehart, & Winston
Goatskin, limited edition of 26, Phantasia; I have "Q"
British edition: Orbit
Japanese edition: Hayakawa Publishing, Inc., 1981
French edition: Nouvelles Editions Opta, 1982, as *Les Ingenieurs De L'Anneau-Monde*
German edition: Bastei Lubbe, 1982, as *Die Ringwelt-Ingenieure*

117. "Future Histories," article for the *Bulletin of the SFWA*, special issue on future histories

118. *The Patchwork Girl*, trade paperback, illustrated, Ace, 1978
Japanese edition: illustrated hardback, data in Japanese
Japanese edition: paper, Tokyo: Tokyo Sogensha Co. Ltd.
Israeli edition: with *Long Arm*, data in Hebrew

119. "From Macrostructures Engineering: Progress Report," *Lunacon 1980 Program Book*

120. "The Green Marauder," *Destinies*, February-March 1980
Anthology, *Dream's Edge*, ed. Terry Carr, Sierra Club Books, 1980
Anthology, *Best Science Fiction Stories of the Year*, ed. Gardner Dozois, 1980
Collection, *Limits* (#151)
Anthology, *Top Science Fiction*, ed. Josh Pachter, Dent
Collection, *Playgrounds of the Mind* (#178)
Sirius (fanzine), broj 145

121. "Retrospective," with Steven Barnes, *Destinies*, Summer 1980
Section from *Dream Park* (#126)
Collection, *Playgrounds of the Mind* (#178)

122. "On the Marching Morons," with Isaac Asimov, *Isaac Asimov's Science Fiction Magazine*, January 1981

123. "The Real Thing," German first publication, 1981, as "Tor Zu Den Sternen"

Isaac Asimov's Science Fiction Magazine, November 1982
Collection, *Limits* (#151)

124. *Oath of Fealty*, with Jerry Pournelle, section in *Omni*, October 1981

125. "Yet Another Modest Proposal: The Roentgen Standard," *Omni*, "Lastword," October 1981
Collection, *Limits* (#151)

126. *Dream Park*, with Steven Barnes
Limited edition with signatures from Phantasia Press
Ace Books, trade, paper, and hardbound Book Club
Italian edition: Milan: Mondadori Fantascienza, as *Parco Dei Sogni*

127. *The Magic May Return*, anthology, ed. by Larry Niven, Ace Books, 1981

128. "War Movie," *Stellar* #7, ed. Judy-Lynn Del Rey
Collection, *Limits* (#151)
Collection, *Playgrounds of the Mind* (#178)

129. "Limits," *Isaac Asimov's Science Fiction Magazine*, September 1981
Anthology, *Aliens and Outworlders*, ed. Shawna McCarthy, Davis, 1983
Collection, *Playgrounds of the Mind* (#178)

130. "The Theory and Practice of Instant Learning," collection, *Niven's Laws* (#141)
Herald-Examiner, Sunday, October 18, 1981

131. *Oath of Fealty*, with Jerry Pournelle, 1981
Limited edition, signatures, from Phantasia Press
Timescape Books (Simon & Schuster/Pocket Books)
British edition: Orbit
Paper: Pocket Fiction (Simon & Schuster/Pocket Books)

132. "Talisman," with Dian Girard, *F&SF*, November 1981
Collection, *Limits* (#151)

Collection, *More Magic* (#153)

133. "The Lion in His Attic," *F&SF*, July 1982
Collection, *Limits* (#151)
Collection, *More Magic* (#153)
Collection, *Playgrounds of the Mind* (#178)

134. "The Wristwatch Plantation," with Sharman Di Vono and Ron Harris, newspaper comic strip set in the Star Trek universe, *Houston Chronicle*, March 1 through July 17, 1982

135. "The Notebooks of Mack Sikes," *SFWA Forum*
Science Fiction Review (fanzine)

136. *The Descent of Anansi* with Steven Barnes, segment in *Analog*, October 1982
Tor, 1982
Orbit/Futura/MacDonald & Co., 1984

137. "Reflex," with Jerry Pournelle, anthology, *There Will Be War*, ed. Jerry Pournelle

138. *De Stranden Van Serius Vier*
Dutch collection of Niven stories, Meulenhoff Science Fiction, 1975

139. "A Teardrop Falls," (Berserker story), *Omni*, June 1983
Collection, *Limits* (#151)
Novel by Fred Saberhagen and others, *Berserker Base*, 1985
Collection, *Playgrounds of the Mind* (#178)

140. *The Integral Trees*, serial, *Analog*, October 1983 through January 1984
Hardback, Del Rey, March 1984
Paperback, February 1985
British edition: Futura Publications, 1985
Dutch edition: Amsterdam: Meulenhoff, 1985, as *De Integraalbomen*
German edition: Bastei Lubbe, 1989, as *Welt In Den Luften*

141. *Niven's Laws*, Owlswick Press, 1984
Principal Speaker's book published for Philcon, 1984

142. "Table Manners," collection, *Niven's Laws* (#141)
Collection, *Limits* (#151), as "Folk Tale"

143. "Niven's Laws," article, collection, *Niven's Laws* (#141)
Collection, *N-Space* (#177A)

144. "Convention Stories," article, collection, *Niven's Laws* (#141)

145. "Staying Rich," article, collection, *Niven's Laws* (#141)

146. "The Theory and Practice of Instant Learning," article, collection, *Niven's Laws* (#141)

147. "If Idi Amin Had Had the Bomb," article, collection, *Niven's Laws* (#141)

148. "In Memoriam: Howard Grote Littlemead," poem, collection, *Niven's Laws* (#141)

149. "Why Men Fight Wars and What You Can Do about It," article, collection, *Niven's Laws* (#141)
Collection, *Playgrounds of the Mind* (#178)

150. "Collaborations," article, collection, *Niven's Laws* (#141)

151. *Limits*, Del Rey Books, February 1985

152. "Equipment, Method, and the Rest," article for *The Science Fiction Source Book*, ed. David Wingrove, 1984

153. *More Magic*, collection, ed. Larry Niven, Berkley Fantasy (Ace), 1984

154. *The Time of the Warlock*, collected Warlock stories, illustrated by Dennis Wolf, Steeldragon Press, hardback, limited, 1984

155. *Footfall*, with Jerry Pournelle, Del Rey (Ballantine), May 1985, Michael Whelan cover
British edition: Victor Gollancz Company, 1985
Bra Spanning, as *Invasion*

156. *Limits* (registered here by mistake)

157. "Tell Me a Story," advice for writers, in *Writers of the Future* #2, 1986
158. *The Smoke Ring*, serial in *Analog*, January thru April 1987
Hardback, Del Rey Books, June 1987
Hardback, MacDonald, 1987
Paper, Del Rey, 1987
159. *The Legacy of Heorot*, with Jerry Pournelle and Steven Barnes, maps by Alexis Wolser
Hardback, Simon & Schuster, July 1987
Paperback, Pocket Books
British edition: Gollancz, 1987
Dutch edition: Uitgeverij Luitingh B.V., 1987, as *Heorot*
160. "The Tale of the Jinni and the Sisters," *Argos SF&F*, Penrhyn Publishing
Anthology, *Arabesques #1*, ed. Susan Shwartz, July 1988, Avon & Pan Books
Collection, *N-Space* (#177A)
161. "The Dreadful White Page," postcard story for Surplus Wyvern Press
Collection, *Playgrounds of the Mind* (#178)
162. "Brenda," anthology, *War World #2*, ed. Jerry Pournelle
New Destinies, Spring 1988
Collection, *N-Space* (#177A)
163. "The Gripping Hand"
Novella-shaped first section of *The Gripping Hand*, novel by Larry Niven and Jerry Pournelle. We tried to get it published as a Marvel graphic. Retitle "Snow Ghost," if we ever get a second shot.
164. "Curse"
?
165. "Next Time," 100-word story for anthology, *The Drabble Project*, April 1988

166. "The Portrait of Daryanree the King," anthology, *More Tales from the Forbidden Planet*
Anthology rights promised for *Arabesques #3*, ed. Susan Shwartz
Collection, *Playgrounds of the Mind* (#178)

167. "The Wishing Game," last tale of the Warlock's companions
Anthology, *Arabesques #2*, ed. Susan Shwartz, Avon, 1989
Collection, *Playgrounds of the Mind* (#178)

168. "Autograph Etiquette"
?

169. Review of *The Prisoner* for *Reason Magazine*, 1987

170. Review of *Against the Fall of Night* and *Great Sky River* for *Reason Magazine*, 1987

171. "The Murder of Halley's Comet," with David Drake, anthology, *The Fleet, Book #3*

172. *Dream Park 2: The Barsoom Project* with Steven Barnes, Ace Books, 1989

173. "The Alien In Our Minds," anthology, *Aliens, The Anthropology of Science Fiction*, ed. George E. Slusser and Eric S. Rabkin, Southern Illinois University Press, 1987
Collection, *N-Space* (#177A)

174. "Criticism," *New Destinies*, ed. James Baen, Spring 1989
Collection, *Playgrounds of the Mind* (#178)

175. *The Man-Kzin Wars #2*, ed. Larry Niven and James Baen, 1989

176. "The Return of William Proxmire," anthology, *What Might Have Been*, ed. Gregory Benford and Martin H. Greenberg, 1989
Requiem, ed. Yoji Kondo, Tor, 1992
Collection, *N-Space* (#177A)

177. "Madness Has Its Place," *Isaac Asimov's Science Fiction Magazine*, June 1991
Analog, June 1990

Anthology, *The Man-Kzin Wars IV,* Baen Books, 1989
Collection, *N-Space* (#177A)

177A. *N-Space*, collection, Tor, 1989

178. *Playgrounds of the Mind*, collection, Tor, 1991

179. *Achilles' Choice*, with Steven Barnes, Tor, 1991
German edition: Bastei Lubbe, paper, 1991, as *Die Wahl Des Achill*

180. *Fallen Angels*, with Jerry Pournelle and Michael Flynn, Baen Books, 1991

181. *The California Voodoo Game (Dream Park 3)*, with Steven Barnes, Del Rey, 1992

182. *Green Lantern: Ganthet's Tale*, graphic novel with John Byrne (script and art)

183. "The Lost Ideas," collection, *Playgrounds of the Mind* (#178)

184. "Ghetto? But I Thought...," collection, *Playgrounds of the Mind* (#178)

185. "Adrienne and Irish Coffee," collection, *Playgrounds of the Mind* (#178)

186. "One Night at the Draco Tavern," script for the 1984 WorldCon Masquerade in Los Angeles
Collection, *Playgrounds of the Mind* (#178)

187. "Trantorcon Report," collection, *Playgrounds of the Mind* (#178)

188. "Comics," collection, *Playgrounds of the Mind* (#178)

189. "The Green Lantern Bible update," 1991, DC, collection, excerpt in *Playgrounds of the Mind* (#178)

190. "The Kiteman," collection, *N-Space* (#177A)

191. "Space," memoir, collection, *N-Space* (#177A)

192. *The Gripping Hand*, with Jerry Pournelle, Pocket Books, hard-cover, 1992. To be published in Great Britain as *The Mote Around Murcheson's Eye*.

ACKNOWLEDGEMENTS

This book could not have been produced without the help of:

Honored Guest Larry Niven, not only for creating the fiction and nonfiction that makes this book possible, but also for delivering material on time, answering questions promptly, and generally providing the model of the professional author (dilettante or no).

Honored Guest Alicia Austin for the beautiful illustrations, and for equally professional attention to deadlines, specifications, and other aesthetic concerns.

Jinx Beers, for professionalism worthy of an Honored Guest.

Tom Whitmore, for bravura bibliographic research, proofreading, and advice.

Peggy Rae Pavlat, for essential information, and for just enough nagging and not too much.

Catherine Campaigne, for design, typesetting, and professional advice.

—Debbie Notkin
editor